Millennium City

Death Comes Uninvited

Disclaimer:
This is a work of fiction. The story, plot and incidents described are all figments of the imagination of the author. The characters of this novel bear no resemblance to any person whatsoever, living or dead.

Published by
Prakash Books India Pvt. Ltd.
1, Ansari Road, Daryaganj,
New Delhi-110 002
Tel.: 91-11-2324 7062-65
sales@prakashbooks.com
www.prakashbooks.com

ISBN: 978 81 7234 372 9

Processed & printed in India by Saurabh Printers Pvt. Ltd.

Millennium City

Death Comes Uninvited

JOYGOPAL PODDER

PRAKASH BOOKS

Contents

Dedication

This book is dedicated to my wife Priti and to my daughters Panvi and Piya – and to the memory of the many fun filled times we have had in the 'Millennium City'.

"Our life is made by the death of others"

Leonardo da Vinci

You've Got Mail

The last thing any average person would expect to see parked in the 'inbox' of his or her e-mail account is the confession of a murderer. A professed serial killer, at that…

Not a nice way to start off a day – reading such a mail.

The words of the e-mail hit Jeevan Mathur like a sledgehammer.

I have killed again. The body is lying in the bedroom of Apartment 45, Astor Green, South City 1. (The Gurgaon Killer)

Jeevan Mathur stared at the computer screen in disbelief. He read the short message, which was typed all in italics, again. And again.

The words refused to change. Or disappear.

It was the subject line of the e-mail, which had drawn Jeevan's attention when he had scanned the 'inbox' of the e-mail account of 'Gurgaon Window' – the local newspaper that he and his wife Pooja together published and edited.

The subject line of the e-mail was typed in capital letters. There were only six words in the subject line – but they hit with the force of a sledgehammer.

I AM BACK WITH ANOTHER KILLING

The sender of the e-mail (in the 'from' box) was simply mentioned as TGK. It was only after reading the contents of the e-mail that Jeevan realised with a shock that, when the sender had typed TGK, he was calling himself (or herself?) 'The Gurgaon Killer' in an abbreviated form.

Jeevan Mathur was tempted to delete the message – write it off as a prank; another example of annoying and useless 'spam' mail, this one in extreme bad taste. What stopped him was the fact that the mail had not lodged in the 'bulk' folder – the usual automatic repository of 'spam' mail – but was deposited in the 'inbox'.

The mail had not been sent to a mass of addressees – like a 'spam' mail. It had apparently been sent exclusively to the e-mail account of 'Gurgaon Window'.

I have killed again. The body is lying in the bedroom of Apartment 45, Astor Green, South City 1. (The Gurgaon Killer)

Jeevan Mathur shivered. The e-mail had put an unexpected burden on his shoulders. What if the mail was not a prank? What if there was *actually a dead body* lying in the bedroom of the apartment that had been specified in the mail? And what if the dead body – if one was actually discovered – was found to be that of a person who had died an unnatural death?

Jeevan took his decision. He acted as he normally did when faced with a crisis. He picked up the phone and called his wife.

The Dead Body

The body was neatly laid out on the bed, face up, head on the pillow. The blood from the wound had dried on the neck – it was caked around the deep gash from which it had spurted.

The throat had been slit elsewhere, not on the bed. That fact was clearly evident from the dried blood – lots of it – spread around the sink and on the floor of the kitchen in this apartment in Astor Green condominium. The body had been dragged to the bedroom – there was a trail of blood leading from the kitchen to near the bed.

Detective Superintendent Avinash Sharma of the Gurgaon Police Crime Branch stared down at the relatively peaceful looking face of the dead woman. The woman's eyes were shut. She would have been no more than thirty years of age, not bad looking – even in horrifying death – and had evidently been a well-groomed young lady. When she had been alive.

The dead woman was fully clothed – in a pink salwar kameez. Only the dupatta was missing from around the neck; hence the wound of the slit throat was clearly visible. This was not a sex crime – the woman had not been molested prior to – or after – her death. Or so it appeared.

Detective Superintendent Avinash Sharma was a battle hardened police officer of forty years of age. Violent death was not new to him. Dealing with murder and killings was his chosen career; viewing dead bodies at crime scenes was a more frequent occurrence in his life. Yet, even he was moved at the sight of this peaceful looking, dead young woman, whose life had been cut short – so suddenly and so violently.

The dead woman was certainly somebody's daughter, probably someone's sister, perhaps somebody's wife or girlfriend, maybe even a child's mother. What right did anybody have to take away her life from her?

As the forensic experts went about their jobs all around him, picking up fingerprints from furniture and fixtures and organizing photographs of the dead woman from different angles, Detective Superintendent Avinash Sharma's attention was suddenly caught by an object lying on the bed, right next to the dead body. He bent down and picked it up.

He held in his hand what looked like a driver's license.

He held the license close to his eyes and stared hard. The face in the photograph that stared back at him was that of a young woman – but it was definitely *not* that of the dead woman lying on the bed…

Searching For Clues

Detective Superintendent Avinash Sharma of the Gurgaon Police Crime Branch studied the hard copy of the e-mail in his hand. He then studied the e-mail displayed on the computer screen. The e-mails were, obviously, identical. He sighed and put down the sheet of paper on the table.

"No clues there," he commented. He looked at Jeevan Mathur and asked: "This TGK fellow – has he, or she, sent a mail to 'Gurgaon Window' before?"

"No, never."

"Have you ever received similar messages under different names – from different senders, not TGK?"

This time, Pooja Mathur responded: "No. This is the first time we've received anything remotely sinister in our mailbox. It was quite a chilling experience to read it in the first instance!"

Detective Sharma studied Pooja Mathur with interest. It was difficult to imagine that anything – much less a mail – would be capable of giving her a chilling experience.

Pooja Mathur was a determined looking young woman of about thirty five years of age who, Avinash Sharma knew, had thrown up a lucrative advertising job to start her local newspaper 'Gurgaon Window' with her husband Jeevan. A mother of two very young daughters, Pooja micro-managed her newspaper and her family with matter-of-fact efficiency – and had developed an enviable reputation in Gurgaon of being able to collect payments from even the most tight-fisted of the newspaper's advertisers in advance of printing their advertisements. No mean feat in a market flooded with cottage industry newspaper and magazine start-ups.

All this Detective Avinash knew because (a) it was his job to investigate the background of the individuals who had tipped off the police about the dead young woman in Apartment 45 of the Aster Green condominium and (b) he was an appreciative and regular reader of 'Gurgaon Window' which was delivered to his house in Sushant Lok 1 every Friday wrapped inside his copy of *The Hindustan Times* newspaper.

"The message was sent from a rediffmail account. The rediffmail records may be able to reveal the details of the person who had registered the e-mail address," observed Jeevan Mathur, wiping his spectacle lenses with his handkerchief.

"No luck there," replied Avinash Sharma. "The e-mail account 'tgk@rediffmail.com' was opened under a false name – I think it was Shah Rukh Salman Khan, if I remember correctly! The killer – if the sender of the mail is indeed the killer – appears to possess a bizarre sense of humour." Avinash took a thankful sip from the hot cup of coffee that had been placed in front of him by Pooja Mathur and then continued. "As expected, the address given in the e-mail account opening particulars was bogus – a veterinary clinic is run from there in the Bandra area of Mumbai by a seventy year old Parsi doctor who has never been to Delhi in his life, much less to this Delhi suburb of Gurgaon."

"Where was the mail sent from?" asked Pooja Mathur.

"Now *that's* an interesting lead," commented Detective Superintendent Avinash Sharma, brightening up a bit. "We've traced the origin of the e-mail with the help of our cyber sleuths. The mail was sent from a cyber café in Super Mart, the shopping complex located in DLF City IV, right here in the middle of new Gurgaon. So, the killer not only murders here, but he also conducts his other operations from Gurgaon. He – or she – could be a local resident."

"Did the sender of the e-mail not produce an identity proof before using the cyber café computer?" asked Jeevan. "That's the rule, isn't it?"

"The cyber café owner says that the customer must have – but he does not remember what it was, or what the person looked like," said Avinash grimly. "The cyber café seems to attract almost a hundred customers every evening and night – so it would be easy for unscrupulous e-mailers to do their work in anonymity."

"What about the dead woman's husband?" queried Jeevan. "Did he supply any leads? Personal enmity or professional rivalry?"

"None. It wasn't easy to talk to the husband – he appears to be completely devastated by his wife's death. Not a very old marriage – they met at work. It was an office romance. The husband, who was at the Leisure Valley park jogging with a friend when the killing took place early morning in his apartment – we've checked his movements – is in a state of shock right now. We'll talk to him in detail, later."

"So there are no clues to work on?" observed Pooja. "No fingerprints or murder weapon?"

"Detective stories and TV serials make our work appear so simple, don't they?" remarked Detective Superintendent Avinash Sharma a bit sarcastically. "No, in real life, killers know all about not leaving evidence like fingerprints and murder weapons at the scene of the crime." He paused and then continued: "There is only one interesting find at the scene of the crime which might help us track down the killer. *This!*" Avinash Sharma held up the driving license he had discovered next to the dead body.

Jeevan Mathur stared hard at the photograph of the girl displayed on the license and reached out with a slightly shaking hand. Puzzled, Avinash Sharma handed the license to Jeevan, who adjusted his spectacles and studied the details printed on the laminated card. He then looked up, his face white.

"It is as I had guessed!" he exclaimed. "This driver's license belongs to a girl who had been killed nine years ago!"

The Real Estate Mogul

Divyansh Malhotra had a talent for recognizing opportunity where others saw nothing. He had seen the potential in the rapidly developing Delhi suburb of Gurgaon – and had leveraged every opportunity he could grab to build a real estate empire that had propelled him right up to the front ranks of Indian businessmen.

He now stood before the imposing gates of the luxury apartment complex, Malhotra Court, built by him and marvelled at the fabulous lifestyle he had made possible for two thousand families.

The four bankers who stood alongside him, also marvelled at the magnificent lifestyle that would now be enjoyed by the residents of Malhotra Court because of the superb location of this apartment complex. The four bankers also marvelled at the absolutely brilliant profits they would be raking in for their respective banks as a result of the great foresight of Divyansh Malhotra – the man who had recognized the potential in this vacant plot of land long before any development had taken place on this stretch of road.

Now, three years after they had reluctantly agreed to help fund this real estate project, the bankers realized and savoured the full power of Divyansh Malhotra's brilliant ability to anticipate the future.

Flanking Malhotra Court, on either side of the apartment complex, were two of the most popular malls and Cineplex's of the National Capital Region – walking distance for the favoured residents of the condominium complex which Divyansh Malhotra had just built and named after himself. Also at walking distance from the imposing gates of Malhotra Court – in fact, right in front of the guard room – was located the new Mall Road metro rail station of the recently inaugurated metro line that connected Gurgaon to every corner of the National Capital Region; every corner of New Delhi and all its suburbs.

Those willing to sell off their Delhi properties at the astronomical prices such houses and apartments of the capital city commanded and settle down in Gurgaon (there were many thousands of such people and families) were equally eager to pay fortunes to purchase apartments at the wonderfully located Malhotra Court condominium complex.

Divyansh Malhotra and his banker partners were now, literally, laughing their way to the bank – their pockets jingling with stupendous profits.

It was time, felt Divyansh, to remind his banker friends that he had not always been so popular with them. It was time, decided Divyansh, to remind his banker friends that they had literally threatened to drag him to court for debt repayment just about an year ago.

Past Crimes

Detective Superintendent Avinash Sharma stared at the computer screen in amazement. Jeevan Mathur had clicked on a link on the *Tribune* newspaper website homepage. It opened up the news report of the killing of Rajshree Mishra in Gurgaon in December 2001.

"It was the tag 'The Gurgaon Killer' on the e-mail that I received that sent me surfing on the internet to track past reports of this self-professed serial killer," said Jeevan Mathur. "The e-mail said that this murderer was *back with another killing* – so I decided to check out if there were reports of TGK killings in the past."

"This is one such report?" asked Avinash Sharma, scanning the nine year old *Tribune* news item displayed on the computer screen.

"Yes," responded Jeevan. "The girl Rajshree Mishra was found dead in the driving seat of her car in the parking lot of Capitol Hotel. Her throat had been slit."

There was a silence as Detective Avinash digested this piece of information.

"Her hand bag was missing – so there was nothing on the young woman to establish her identity and residence," continued Jeevan after a short pause. "The Gurgaon police were able to establish her identity a couple of days later by matching her with the Missing Person report filed by her family."

Pooja Mathur interjected: "The manager of the local office of the *Tribune* newspaper had found a packet on the reception desk. It had a note saying that a woman's body would be found in the Capitol Hotel parking lot. The note was not handwritten – it was typed. Typewriters were still in common use those days. The name at the bottom of the note was – 'The Gurgaon Killer'. Since several killings in the past few years had been attributed to 'The Gurgaon Killer', the local police took the note very seriously and quickly rushed to the spot mentioned – and as predicted in the note, discovered the body with the slit throat."

There was another silence.

Detective Superintendent Avinash Sharma studied the photograph of the woman, Rajshree Mishra, featured in the *Tribune* news report of nine years ago and then looked at the photograph on the driving license in his hand.

The faces on both photographs were identical. The driving license carried the name Rajshree Mishra. The license had clearly belonged to the woman who had been killed and left in the Capitol Hotel parking lot.

"So the killer left this license at the scene of his – or her – *latest* crime to establish his/her connection with the past killing," commented Avinash Sharma, his face grim. "We *do* appear to be dealing with a serial killer..."

"'The Gurgaon Killer' appears to have resurfaced," added Pooja Mathur.

Calling The Shots

Divyansh Malhotra surveyed the four eager faces in front of him with satisfaction. These four very senior bank executives, each representing one of the biggest private sector banks in the country, were literally crying to eat of his hands.

He would give them a lot to chew on today.

"My friends, I have delivered as I had promised!" he announced completely unnecessarily. He had been rubbing this point home for many days already.

"You surely have, Mr. Malhotra," responded Umesh Narang warmly. Umesh was Sr. Vice President of Tomorrow Bank, India's second largest private sector bank. Umesh had been in the forefront of those of Divyansh Malhotra's creditors who had tried to pressurize the real estate developer to file for bankruptcy just about a year ago.

Divyansh merely smiled at Umesh and did not respond.

Satyajit Mukherjee, Sr. Vice President of United India Bank, India's third largest private sector bank, was equally effusive with his praise. "You have the Midas touch, Mr. Malhotra," said Satyajit Mukherjee. "Whatever you touch turns to gold!"

Divyansh Malhotra finally responded: "Your confidence in my abilities overwhelms me, my friends," he said with a large smile. "But this confidence was very much missing just a year ago – when I needed it most..."

An uncomfortable silence fell in the meeting room. You could have heard the proverbial pin drop in Divyansh Malhotra's plush office complex on the fifth floor of the six storied Nehru Park building located on Gurgaon's prestigious M.G. Road – just a stone's throw away from the latest jewel in the crown of the Malhotra real estate empire, Malhotra Court.

Divyansh continued: "I am not one to hold any grudges, gentlemen, but how can I forget that if you had got your way, this very successful project called Malhotra Court might have been abandoned half way. And I would have been bankrupt!"

Umesh Narang stirred uncomfortably in his seat. A plump man in his mid forties, he was not taking this mini dressing down too well. Beads of sweat had begun to form on his forehead. "Let's bury the past, Mr. Malhotra," he requested. "You have proven your point."

"I had to practically mortgage my soul to save my project," Divyansh reminded Umesh with a slight edge in his voice. "Only I know what hell you guys have made me go through to see my dream project through!"

The atmosphere became tense. The discomfort amongst the bankers was palpalable.

Divyansh Malhotra kept quiet as the bearers served tea and biscuits to his guests and him. After the servers had exited from the meeting room, he continued: "My biggest projects are ahead of me – I have only just hit my stride. I will be happy to continue with your banks as my partners, but from now on our partnership will be on more equal terms, if you gentlemen don't mind!"

The four bankers looked at each other with puzzled expressions. What price would the real estate tycoon, flush with his great success, demand from them for his continued business?

They didn't have to wait long to find out. "Henceforth, I will take project funding from your banks not in the form of loans but as equity," Divyansh announced. "I would expect my bank partners to purchase part ownership of my projects."

The bankers were stunned. Then, one by one, as they mentally analyzed Divyansh Malhotra's proposition, they began to admire the real estate developer's business acumen and foresight once again. This man was leveraging his recent business success to ensure that he would no longer need to raise capital for his projects as a creditor. His financers would have to come on board as equal partners – they would profit from the successful projects but would also share losses in case a development did not meet the business objectives.

Only a businessman like Divyansh Malhotra, basking in his recent glory and, admittedly, with a string of successful real estate developments in the past, could command such terms.

The four bankers knew that they could not afford to lose such a profit-making partner to other rival banks.

They would bite the bait.

"Can we get an idea of the projects you have planned next?" asked Satyajit Mukherjee.

"Certainly!" smiled Divyansh Malhotra. Picking up the receiver of the intercom, he summoned his project managers, who were waiting in an adjoining room with the blueprints of his next real estate ventures. He knew that he had won the day. His dream projects would now get launched with minimum financial risk and burden on his own shoulders – his banks would pick up the tab as co-owners. He was well on his way to seeing his name on some of the grandest and biggest buildings in India's millennium city – Gurgaon.

It was a far cry from his pathetic situation in the cramped and hot Gurgaon court room that he had stood in as an accused criminal in a property cheating case, nine years ago.

All because the real estate developer whose affordable housing project that he had marketed had fled with his clients' money, leaving him to face the music.

Well, he had got the last word even then – as he had now. The cheat Rajeev Senapati had been finally caught, as a result of Divyansh Malhotra's dogged and desperate efforts.

Rajeev Senapati had been convicted and sent, nine years back, to where he belonged. To jail.

Divyansh had won a pardon – he had been found to have been manipulated by the cheat Rajeev Senapati. It had still taken Divyansh many hard years of toil and stress to pay off the clients who had lost their life's savings to the cheat Rajeev Senapati.

It was Divyansh Malhotra's greatest wish and prayer that Rajeev bloody Senapati would rot in – and die in – jail.

The Media Attacks

The atmosphere at the venue of the press conference was electrifying. A serial killer was at large – one who had resurfaced after almost a decade. Gurgaon, the millennium city, was under siege.

Detective Superintendent Avinash Sharma was hard pressed to contain the situation.

The residents of Astor Green, the apartment complex in which the murdered woman had been found, had lost no time in spreading the news of their neighbour's gristly death to friends and relatives. This was the age of instant communication via mobile phone and internet. The media were quick to sniff out the news – and demanded an immediate official update.

Avinash Sharma was the investigating officer. He was deputed to face the media and answer their queries.

The venue was overrun with media. TV and news trucks surrounded the Gurgaon police headquarters building outside; inside the briefing hall, thick black cable stretched over tables and chairs and in every possible direction. TV channel and cable reporters, comfortably rumpled from waist down and impeccably dressed and groomed above it, their faces caked with make-up, stood inside circles of white-hot light and filed their first reports into the cameras. The head table, with Avinash Sharma sitting prominently in the centre, was featured in every camera frame, even if the TV channel or cable reporter hogged the foreground.

The reporters from the print media crowded around the head table, jostling for space, their microphones thrust towards Avinash – the star of the afternoon. The still photographers clicked away incessantly, flashbulbs popping non-stop. The glare was almost blinding.

The atmosphere was electrifying – an air of palpable tension sparked in the room. After all, there was about to be a police versus media face-off.

There were, of course, policemen around in large numbers – but they had clear instructions not to try any heavy-handed antics to keep the media representatives in order. The murder was the topic of the hour and it had to remain so – no police top brass wanted the press to leave the media briefing venue with stories about police high-handedness. The focus would need to remain firmly on the agenda of the press meet – the Astor Green murder.

The policemen at the venue of the press meet kept an arm's length from the crowd of media persons. Avinash, for all practical purposes, was on his own.

He answered the first obvious question. Was the young woman's murder the handiwork of a serial killer?

"We do not know," said Avinash Sharma truthfully. "We were tipped off by an e-mail that was signed by a person who called himself – or herself – 'The Gurgaon Killer'.

Sensation.

The press representatives, like Jeevan and Pooja Mathur before them, had done their homework. Their informants inside police headquarters had already tipped them off about the e-mail to 'Gurgaon Window'. "Isn't this the same killer who terrorized Gurgaon a decade ago?" asked an earnest looking young lady reporter from a leading TV news channel.

"Careful, careful..." thought Avinash to himself. He steeled himself to choose his words with care. A wrong word or sentence now, on national television, could spark off a tidal wave of fear in and around Gurgaon. He would need to play it cool.

"We do not have any reason to believe so, as yet," stated Avinash Sharma as firmly as he could. He continued quickly, without letting the numerous attempts to interrupt him prevail: "There was, admittedly, a series of killings ten to fifteen years ago attributed – but never proved – to the same person who called himself or herself, 'The Gurgaon Killer' in messages sent to the police and the press. But all that stopped about nine or ten years ago. This murder need not be linked to the murders of a decade back."

It was not that easy to put off a media pack standing on the threshold of a sensational story. A middle aged veteran of a thousand press conferences spoke up. "How do you explain," asked the white haired press reporter from the nation's largest circulation daily newspaper, "the fact that not only was the e-mail directing you to the body signed in the same name as the earlier serial killer but also that the same method of sending a message to announce the murder was used, as was the trademark of the old serial killer?"

The crucial question had been asked. The hall fell silent. Everybody waited with bated breath for the man in the spotlight to deny the obvious.

Avinash drew a deep breath. All this speculation had to be cut short. The media would still be frothing with speculation with or without his inputs – but he needed to get on with his job and catch the killer of the young woman in Astor Green condominium. This media briefing was an essential part of his job – but up to a point. His job was to catch murderers – not contribute to media frenzy.

"There has been a murder and the murderer has to be caught," said Avinash, as emphatically as he could. "Right now the investigation is in the very early stages – it is not possible to shed any light on who committed the crime. An attempt has been made to copy an earlier trademark messaging method – but whether there was a serial killer at work in Gurgaon ten years ago has also never been resolved. It is easy to copy something to try and divert investigation. But we will not be diverted. Give us some time – and we will apprehend the murderer. It is extremely premature to state that a serial killer has re-surfaced – where was this person for the last nine years? Please let the investigation take its course – we will catch the murderer and will immediately inform you when we do so."

With that, Detective Superintendent Avinash Sharma stood up and quickly walked out of the hall, followed by his assistants and some policemen, completely ignoring the protestations and shouted questions of the crowd of press reporters he had left behind.

Nestled safely in his jacket pocket was the driving license of the murdered girl of nine years ago – that had been found next to the body of the young woman found murdered only a few hours ago. Both bodies had been found as a consequence of a message sent by a person signing off as 'The Gurgaon Killer'.

The discovery of the nine year old driving license next to the dead body in the bedroom in Astor Green condominium was a piece of information that had not been divulged to the press. Jeevan and Pooja Mathur had been sworn to secrecy about it.

If the media representatives and journalists had found out about this mysterious common link with the earlier dead woman– Avinash Sharma knew that he would not have been able to end the press conference so easily…

A Deadly Killer Returns

Detective Superintendent Avinash Sharma surveyed the reports spread out in front of him with some degree of trepidation. The reports had originated from two sources – Gurgaon police archives and the office of 'Gurgaon Window'. The first report had been prepared by police researchers. The second by Jeevan and Pooja Mathur, the intrepid editors of Gurgaon's leading local newspaper.

Both told the same story. Between the years 1994 and 2001, someone calling himself – or herself – 'The Gurgaon Killer' had committed an estimated six known murders in and around what is today known as the Millennium City of India.

Four of the victims of the alleged serial killer had been young women in their twenties and thirties.

Rajshree Mishra, the young woman whose dead body had been found in her car in the parking lot of Capitol Hotel, had been the last known victim of 'The Gurgaon

Killer' – until the dead body in Astor Green Condominium had surfaced.

Detective Inspector Ramesh Uppal, an earnest looking police officer of thirty five years of age and Avinash's lieutenant for the last two years, adjusted his spectacles, cleared his throat and said: "Sir, all the facts point to the inevitable conclusion that the serial killer has re-surfaced. The victims of the earlier murders were mostly young women. So was Geetanjali Mehta, the latest victim. All bodies were found after a tip off from the supposed murderer."

Avinash Sharma nodded his head. "True, very true. But where did the alleged murderer disappear for nine years? And why the sudden reappearance? Is the new killer the same as the old one? Or is someone trying to mislead us – attempting to send us searching in the wrong direction?"

"Could be the latter option, of course," conceded Ramesh Uppal. "However, if – and right now it is, of course, a big if – there *is* a serial killer at large, then we have a serious crisis on our hands!"

"*Every* murder is a serious crisis, my friend," Avinash quickly reminded Ramesh. "Geetanjali Mehta's murder is a crisis by itself, whether committed by a serial killer or a first timer. Her life was taken unnaturally and violently. We must track down the killer, irrespective of whether the murderer is a serial killer or not."

"Of course!" responded Ramesh hastily.

"Let's also remember that once a person has killed another human being it tends to become a habit," observed the seasoned police officer Avinash Sharma. "Geetanjali Mehta's murderer must be tracked down as much as to ensure that he or she gets punished for the crime but also to prevent a killer from being at large and posing a danger to other lives."

"We will need to investigate this as a stand-alone murder…"

"Absolutely! The danger of walking down the serial killer route is that we will tend to ignore the obvious suspects."

"You mean the husband?"

"Yes – and the servants. Or some past or current lover. Or a burglar. Anything is possible. We must begin unraveling Geetanjali Mehta's life immediately for clues!"

"And the past murders?"

"That's also a line of investigation that we cannot ignore. After all, the e-mail was signed off with the name 'The Gurgaon Killer'. We will need to study the investigation reports of each of the six murders of a decade ago, attributed to the serial killer, and see what story they have to tell..."

"You think that there could be clues to the murder of Geetanjali Mehta in the investigation reports of the earlier murders?" asked Ramesh Uppal, looking slightly surprised. "I thought that you were ruling out the possibility of the current murderer being the same as the one who committed the earlier killings."

"I am ruling out nothing! I am only saying that we do not jump to any conclusions regarding the involvement of a serial killer without making proper investigations. We may be dealing with a 'copy cat' murderer for all we know – in which case, the earlier murders would also need to be studied."

"You mean that the murderer of today could be copying the methodology of the earlier killer..."

"Yes, that's what I mean," responded Avinash Sharma. "I also want us to always keep in mind the fact that, whether the murderer of Geetanjali Mehta was involved in the past killings or not, the alleged serial killer of the 1994 – 2001 murders was never caught..."

Ramesh looked thoughtful. "You mean he – or she – might still be around? A potential danger to the public at large?"

"Yes – a very real and a very grave danger..."

The New Project

Divyansh Malhotra sat in the tiny but neat drawing room located on the first floor of the twenty year old Karmayogi Housing Society apartment complex situated at the intersection of Gurgaon's IFFCO Chowk with National Highway 8.

He sipped tea from a sturdy mug and surveyed his surroundings.

The drawing room could barely seat six around the modest looking centre table. The three seater sofa and the accompanying single seaters were equally modest. The rug on the floor was weather beaten and had clearly survived several generations of feet. The walls were adorned with family photographs in cheap frames. Children and grand-children stared down with clear hostility from the framed photographs, counterbalancing the self-conscious smiles on the faces of the adults who also adorned the pictures along with these younger members of the greater family.

The couple who shared the drawing room with Divyansh Malhotra and his Commercial Director Rani Suri, were in their late sixties – more than twenty years older than their guests. The children had long grown up and fled to greener pastures (read: foreign shores) leaving their ageing parents to spend their twilight years in a lonely and purposeless existence amidst memories and relics of better and happier times. The husband had long retired from government service – and the elderly coupled eked out a lower middle class existence on his meager pension and equally meager savings.

Not a pretty picture – but the couple sitting in front of him exuded an aura of quiet dignity and an air of calm and composure that Divyansh was forced to envy.

He also envied the unbelievably prime location that the Karmayogi Housing Society apartment complex had become as a result of the almost miraculous developments that had taken place around it over the years.

Mr. and Mrs. Sharma, the couple who owned this apartment, were now worth over a couple of crore rupees as a result of the value of their property, as were the other owner residents of Karmayogi Housing Society apartment complex.

Divyansh was visiting Mr. and Mrs. Sharma to not only enlighten them on how wealthy they actually were as a result of the value of their property – but to also convince them to encash on this wealth, along with the other apartment owners, by selling out to him.

The elderly gentleman was named Rameshwar Sharma. He held the hand of his wife seated next to him in a gesture of companiable affection that Rani Suri found greatly endearing. She stole a glance at the hand of her boss, Divyansh Malhotra, which was still holding the mug of tea, and sighed mentally.

Rameshwar Sharma cleared his throat and said: "It is not as if we *need* money…"

"I am not in any way saying that," responded Divyansh hastily. "All I am saying is that your property has appreciated greatly in value as a result of the remarkable growth of Gurgaon – and selling it now, and convincing the other fifty nine families here to sell, will make you all very rich. Your standard of living can go up considerably, if you want it to."

"We will also lose our home," commented Gita Sharma. "After all these years of living in our own apartment, it will not be possible for us to adjust to rented accommodation."

"No madam, you will not have to shift into rented accommodation," replied Rani Suri earnestly. "The value of your apartment – if it is sold to us as a block deal with all the other fifty nine apartments of Karmayogi Housing Society – is over two crore rupees. That is because this location has acquired significant commercial value as a result of its proximity to the new expressway and the fact that the IFFCO Chowk intersection falls at the end of the road on which all the new malls are located."

"We know all that, my dear," said Rameshwar Sharma gently. "But you haven't addressed my wife's concern. Where will we go if we sell our home to you or anybody else? We do not like the idea of shifting to a rented accommodation and being at the mercy of the whims of a landlord at this stage in our lives."

"Precisely, sir," responded Rani, not the least bit offended at the interruption. The elderly couple had a genuine concern, which needed to be addressed. Divyansh Malhotra and Rani Suri had come to this meeting prepared to address this concern. "A brand new apartment, twice the size of this one and located in a more peaceful but well settled part of new Gurgaon, will cost you around rupees one crore. We will pay as an advance to you – and to all the other families, if you all sell to us together in one bulk deal – sixty percent of our purchase price. This will enable you to purchase a new apartment and shift into it *before* handing over possession of this apartment to us."

There was a long silence as Mr. and Mrs. Sharma digested this piece of information. They elderly couple finally looked at each other. Geetanjali Sharma nodded very slightly to her husband.

Rameshwar Sharma looked at Divyansh Malhotra, then at Rani Suri and then back at the real estate tycoon. "And what, exactly, is your purchase price offer?" he finally asked.

Divyansh responded. "Rupees two crores and ten lakhs for each of the sixty apartments in Karmayogi Housing Society complex. This offer is conditional to all owners selling to us in one bulk deal. That is why we have come to you – as President of the Resident's Welfare Association, you have the stature and respect here to be able to convince the other owners of the value of our offer."

Rani Suri stepped in to support her boss. "The market value of each apartment, on a standalone basis, is about rupees one crore and sixty lakhs. That is because other purchasers only look at the apartments here from the point of view of residential living – and value the flats in relation to comparable apartments in other locations in terms of size and proximity to essential facilities like markets and hospitals. Your apartments are not very big – only about fourteen hundred square feet. Only small families will show and interest to buy here. But such issues are not important to us. We are valuing the entire complex from a commercial point of view – and are, therefore, offering a premium of fifty lakhs for each apartment. We will build a mall here and make our profits on commercial terms. I think you and the other apartment owners will realise that our offer is giving you an opportunity to encash your property at a very big profit!"

Rameshwar Sharma swallowed slightly. The sums that were being spoken of were a bit beyond his comprehension. "All this is a bit difficult for us to understand," he said. "Why should we take so much trouble on our heads in this old age? First of all you want us to convince our neighbours to sell together. Then you want us to shift to another home. Why should we bother? "

"First of all, sir, you are not old," responded Rani Suri warmly. "Mrs. Sharma and you have many more enjoyable years together ahead of you, of that I am sure. But you need spare money – lots of it – to enjoy life, to be able to travel, to be able to visit your children and grandchildren who are abroad. Also, I am sure that it becomes difficult to accommodate your children and grandchildren in this small apartment when they come visiting. Just imagine how comfortable they will feel if your new home is double the size of this one!"

Rani had hit the nail on the head. She saw a reaction in Gita Sharma's face.

"She is right," Gita Sharma told her husband, straightening up in her chair. "I have begun to realize that one of the reasons that our children have reduced their holiday visits to us is that they find this apartment too congested – particularly for their own growing children."

"Think also of the other families in this complex," said Divyansh Malhotra to Rameshwar Sharma. "Our offer may come to them as a very pleasurable bonanza. Many of your neighbours may be in debt. Many may need large funds to further their children's education. Some may want to start businesses. A thirty percent premium on their apartments over existing market price, which is our offer for a bulk purchase of all the apartments of Karmayogi Society together, may be exactly the kind of bonanza they need at this point in their lives. All you have to do is get them together and ask them on our behalf!"

Rameshwar Sharma smiled. "You both work together very well as a team. Now I understand why you, Mr. Malhotra, have come yourself to talk to us – and not left the job to some manager in your organization. Miss Suri and you have done a very good job of convincing us."

Rani smiled at the compliment and looked at her boss, who studiously ignored her.

Rani sighed inwardly and then responded to Rameshwar Sharma. "Thank you. We have more to offer. Our organization will not only advance you and the other families enough funds to relocate to newer and larger accommodation but we will also actively assist in locating suitable apartments and arranging the purchase on your behalf. We will also help out in all the shifting activities. We will ensure that your move is as comfortable as it can be."

"That is very generous of you," replied Rameshwar Sharma. "But we have not agreed to sell, as yet..."

Divyansh Malhotra and Rani Suri looked at each other confused. Before they could say anything, however, Rameshwar Sharma continued: "We must, first, settle the price."

"But we've told you our offer for your apartment – for *each* of the apartments here," said Divyansh. "Its rupees two crores and ten lakhs."

"Even after all that you have said, your offer may not be attractive enough for me to convince all my fellow owners to sell out to you together," replied Rameshwar Sharma, leaning forward. "I think that a fifty percent premium to what you say is the current market price may be a better and more convincing offer..."

His words were met by a shocked silence. Divyansh Malhotra and Rani Suri quickly looked at each other with speculation in their eyes. Rameshwar Sharma certainly had all his faculties well preserved and well oiled. There was nothing outdated in his ability to surprise and to negotiate.

With a resigned expression, Divyansh leaned forward and got down to the task of negotiating…

Business Rivalry

Jagdeesh Ruia was seething with rage. That upstart Divyansh Malhotra had upstaged him again. He slapped the table with the palm of his hand and glared at his quaking managers.

"How did he get there *first*?" asked Jagdeesh Ruia, almost shouting.

Naresh Kumar, Director Operations at Ruia Builders and Developers (RBD) flinched and answered: "Rani Suri tipped off Divyansh Malhotra about the opportunity. She had been scouting around on NH 8 for locations to build a mall – and came across the Karmayogi Housing Society apartment complex. It was never considered as a potential location for a mall until Rani Suri talked to her boss about the possibility of acquiring it and tearing it down to make way for a new mall."

"Even I had thought of that possibility!" exclaimed Jagdeesh Ruia.

"Yes, sir, you did," quickly responded Naresh Kumar. "But they thought it first – and acted as soon as they firmed up the idea."

Jagdeesh Ruia brooded. Finally he asked: "Are the apartment owners selling out?"

"Yes sir."

"At what price?"

"The offer made was rupees two crore ten lakhs per apartment. The ask was rupees two crore forty lakhs. I think both sides finally settled at rupees two crore thirty lakhs – a forty three percent premium over current market price."

"Does Divyansh Malhotra possess the funds to carry out this ambitious venture?"

"Yes, sir!" replied the Finance Director, Piyush Aggarwal. "His banks are backing him all the way in this mall venture. In fact, they are backing Divyansh Malhotra as equity partners and not lenders – so he has minimal personal risk."

Jagdeesh Ruia brooded further. "Do you realize the kind of fabulous profits Divyansh Malhotra will make once the new mall is constructed and he is ready to sell?"

"Yes sir," said Naresh Kumar. "In fact, if he wants to, he need not even invest in the construction. He can sell his shops well in advance, at a slightly lower price than what he would command when the mall is completed, and still make huge profits."

"And once again he will have a landmark building in Gurgaon named after him," snarled Jagdeesh Ruia.

His managers kept quiet. There was no need to risk provoking an already enraged lion with any unnecessary comment…

Finally, Jagdeesh Ruia looked away from the table lamp that he had been glaring at and eyed his managers who were standing in front of his desk. He had not asked them to be seated. "Have all the apartment owners signed their respective sale agreements?" he asked.

It was Naresh Kumar who once again answered. "I think it is happening in two or three lots. It's difficult to get all the owners together in one place all at the same time. Some are not even residents at the complex – they have rented out their apartments and live themselves in some other city. The logistics involved in the exercise of block purchase has involved getting the owners together in two or three different groups on two or three different occasions."

Jagdeesh Ruia froze his Director Operations with a cold look. "You have not answered my question," he said. "Have *all* the apartment owners signed their respective sale agreements?" Jagdeesh Ruia repeated. "If even one does not sign, this deal is useless to Divyansh Malhotra – and we can move in with a better offer."

"I will find out if some apartment owners of Karmayogi Housing Society have still not signed," said Naresh Kumar quickly, not quite sure what was playing in the mind of his boss.

"Yes, please do so," said Jagdeesh Ruia softly. "Do not delay giving me this information – I would like to know in an hour." He picked up the decorative knife lying on his desk and began playing thoughtfully with the pointed end as his managers filed quietly out of the room. The sharp end of the knife accidentally pricked his forefinger, but Jagdeesh Ruia did not flinch as a drop of blood spurted out from the cut. He merely smiled...

Huda City Metro Station

One day I will go mad, thought Rani Suri as she reversed her Honda Accord into the empty parking bay between a Maruti Ritz and a Mahindra Scorpio at the HUDA City Centre Metro Station in Gurgaon, *and you alone will be responsible for it Divyansh Malhotra, my dear boss!*

As she walked quickly to the main entrance of the metro station and then strode through the metal detector, Rani Suri wondered why men, especially highly intelligent men like Divyansh Malhotra, were so blind.

She collected her laptop bag and handbag from the security machine conveyor belt (had they ever detected *anything* through these x-ray machines installed in the metro stations, so far?) and swiped her metro rail smart card on the sensor at the entry point to the inner sanctum of the station (yes, even *she*, Rani Suri, Commercial Director of the leading real estate development company Malhotra Buildwell, carried a metro rail smart card for emergency public transport travel).

As she cruised up the escalator leading to the boarding and disembarking platforms, Rani Suri wondered how and when she would ever be able to make her boss realize that she was in love with him. And had been in love with him for twelve long years...

The 11 am train drew up to the platform just as she got off the escalator. Rani Suri shrugged off her thoughts and brought her mind to the task at hand. She quickly entered the train compartment closest to her and sat down on an empty bench.

Rani had driven from her office in the Cosmo Tower on NH 8, right opposite the 32nd Milestone recreational complex, to the HUDA City Metro Station, to save on essential time. Her Legal Manager, the young and very capable Deepika Khera, was travelling from the offices of the law firm Gupta and Sinha, located in Delhi's Connaught Place, all the way to Gurgaon on the metro train and she was carrying with her the ten sale agreements for the last ten remaining flats in Karmayogi Housing Society apartment complex which remained to be signed. That morning, Deepika had also parked her car at the HUDA City Metro Station and had caught the 9 am train to Connaught Place. She had thus cleverly beaten the rush hour traffic in time to reach the offices of Gupta and Sinha and pick up the ten sale agreements which had been prepared overnight by the law firm staff.

Deepika was now on her way back to Gurgaon. Rani Suri would meet her almost half way, at Qutub Minar Metro Station, as planned, and study the agreements on the way back to HUDA City Centre Metro Station to check for any flaws and make corrections where necessary.

This was good time management planning – something Rani had become an expert at while working under the mercurial Divyansh Malhotra – and had been made necessary because Rameshwar Sharma, the President of the Karmayogi Housing Society

Resident's Welfare Association, had managed only at the very last minute and after a lot of effort, culminating the previous evening, to assemble the last ten flat owners for sale agreement signing at the society premises. The signing was scheduled this day at 12.30 pm, just before lunchtime. One of the owners was travelling down from Chandigarh. Another was coming from Jaipur. Both wanted to return to their respective homes by end of day.

Time was, therefore, at a premium. Rani Suri had tried to cut down the delays that could have occurred due to travel time. Deepika would not have to go all the way to the Malhotra Buildwell office to deliver the sale agreements, nor would she need to deliver them to Rani at the Karmayogi apartments. Rani would meet her half way on her journey back to Gurgaon, on the metro train itself – and gain additional time to study the papers.

Rani and Deepika would then drive to Karmayogi Housing Society apartment complex straight from the HUDA City Metro Station. They would hopefully arrive in time for the 12.30 pm scheduled signing of the last ten sale agreements. The ten apartment owners would be waiting – or so Rameshwar Sharma has assured.

Rani Suri had not, of course, factored in a murderer and a killing in her detailed planning…

The Second Message

The e-mail was sent to the address of 'Gurgaon Window' at 9 am in the morning.

Jeevan and Pooja Mathur did not know this – they did not start work before 10 am.

It was the SMS which alerted Jeevan Mathur. The SMS had been sent to the cellphones of both Jeevan and Pooja Mathur. Jeevan's cellphone happened to be switched on – and he noticed the message lodged in the phone's inbox at 9.20 am, after he had returned home from his morning jog.

The message was sent from an unknown number. It simply read: "Check your e-mail inbox for details of the latest body."

The result was instantaneous. Jeevan shouted out to Pooja to join him in the 'Gurgaon Window' office located on the ground floor of their modest house. He rushed to the computer installed on his desk, switched it on and logged on to the magazine's yahoo mail account.

Sure enough, the mail was lodged in the inbox. The sender of the e-mail (in the 'from' box) was simply mentioned – as in the earlier mail – as TGK. The mail had been sent from the now familiar id 'tgk@rediffmail.com'.

The subject line of the e-mail was typed in capital letters – as had been the earlier message. It was, as per the now familiar pattern, simply worded – but called for an immediate reading of the contents of the mail.

CHECK THE METRO TRAIN AT
CHATTARPUR FOR THE NEXT BODY

Pooja had joined Jeevan by now and watched as her husband clicked open the e-mail message. The contents were chilling.

The woman will be alive when the train leaves Qutub Minar station at 11.30 am. She will be dead when the train arrives at Chattarpur station. (The Gurgaon Killer)

Pooja Mathur grabbed her phone and speed dialed Detective Superintendent Avinash Sharma.

Between Two Stations

Rani Suri arrived at Qutub Minar Metro Station at 11.20 am. She quickly switched platforms, cruising down one escalator and going up another, and then waited impatiently for the 11.30 am train to come in from Delhi.

Also at 11.20 am, two police jeeps and one ambulance raced into the Qutub Minar Metro Station parking area. Detective Superintendent Avinash Sharma, Detective Inspector Ramesh Uppal and a posse of policemen raced up to the platform on which the incoming train from Delhi would be arriving.

Their objective was not to discover a dead body – but to prevent a murder…

Another posse of policemen, along with another ambulance, was stationed at Chattarpur Metro Station. Similar contingents were stationed at every station in the route all the way till HUDA City Centre Metro Station.

Avinash Sharma had moved very fast and very efficiently.

As the 11.30 am train pulled into the platform, Rani Suri looked curiously at the policemen spread out around her. There appeared to be some practice drill in progress, she thought. She shrugged her shoulders and boarded the nearest compartment.

The train was not very congested at this time of the day. In fact, several benches were empty. As the compartment doors closed shut and the train began moving, Rani dialed Deepika's number. The phone at the other end rang but was not answered.

Frowning slightly, Rani deliberated whether to move to the right or left in search of Deepika. She mentally tossed a coin – and turned to the left.

On such spur of the moment decisions lives and deaths are determined.

Rani brushed past a man who looked like a senior police officer and went into the next compartment, the one on her left. She immediately spotted Deepika Khera. The young woman was slouched in her seat, her briefcase – the one which was supposed to contain the sale agreements – protectively handcuffed to her right wrist in the time honoured practice dictated by security experts.

Breathing a quick sigh of relief, Rani strode up to the bench on which Deepika was sitting – rather slouching – careful not to lose her balance in the fast moving train, which was rapidly nearing Chattarpur Metro Station.

"Hi, Deepika," began Rani – and then stopped. Something was not right. Deepika Khera did not look well. Her eyes were shut and her face was sunk into her chest.

And then Rani Suri noticed the blood. It was oozing out of the right side of Deepika's body. A small pool of blood was slowly forming on the bench right beside the young woman.

Then Rani saw the knife protruding out of the side of Deepika Khera's body…

She screamed.

Panic

The visitor's area of the emergency wing of Gurgaon's Max Hospital was crowded with policemen and press reporters. The media representatives were hungry for information – but none was provided. A tight cordon of policemen surrounded Rani Suri, Divyansh Malhotra and Avinash Sharma.

Divyansh held Rani's hands in a tight grip. He looked very concerned – for the well-being of Deepika, who was battling for her life inside one of the hospital's operation theatres, and also for the well-being of Rani, who was thoroughly shaken from her ordeal.

"Will – will she live?" asked Rani between sobs.

"The doctors are trying their best," assured Divyansh. He looked askingly at Avinash.

"The murderer appeared to have been caught by surprise at the sudden police presence," said Avinash. "His prior warning backfired on him. He did not get the opportunity to strike Deepika as hard and as forcefully as he would have liked to. He must have been in a hurry to get off at Qutub Minar Metro Station. Deepika has been badly wounded – but should survive."

Rani stopped shaking. She still held on to Divyansh's hands.

"The presence of the ambulance and the doctor at the Chattarpur Metro Station probably also contributed to saving Deepika's life – since she got immediate medical attention," commented Divyansh. "That was good thinking, Superintendent!"

Avinash Sharma did not comment, but looked up as a doctor broke the cordon of policemen surrounding them. "Any news, doctor?" he asked.

"The patient is safe," announced Dr. Johri of Max Hospital with a tired smile. "She will live."

Commissioner of Gurgaon Police, Rajender Saxena shook his head as he surveyed the newspapers placed in front of him and observed: "The situation is fast getting out of control. The media is irresponsibly feeding a panic wave in Gurgaon with reports of a serial killer at large in the area. We have to deliver some concrete results quickly!"

"The investigations cannot be compressed, sir," commented Detective Superintendent Avinash Sharma. "The enquiries are on. We have some clues."

"You have some clues to the serial killer?" asked Rajender Saxena surprised.

"I would not say that, sir. But we *do* have some leads in the matter of the Astor Green killing…"

"When will these 'leads' as you call them help you catch the murderer?"

"I hope soon."

"Then get a move on, man. The pressure on us is mounting by the day. The Gurgaon killings are becoming a national issue.

Once the politicians jump on the bandwagon – the whole thing will become a circus!"

"I understand that, sir, but it is difficult to stay one step ahead of the killer."

"If you cannot prevent – then solve. Either way, the murderer must be caught! Do your job!"

"Yes, sir!"

The Telephone Call

Gulshan Mehta was thirty years old – about the same age as his murdered wife. Right now he looked several years older. His face was unshaven. His eyes were bloodshot and swollen. He looked devastated.

Geetanjali Mehta had been murdered several days ago, but her husband was still grieving.

Detective Superintendent Avinash Sharma and Detective Inspector Ramesh Uppal sat in front of Gulshan Mehta in the latter's smart drawing room in Apartment 45, Astor Green Condominium, South City 1, Gurgaon.

Jeevan Mathur had come to this meeting as per the request of Avinash Sharma. He sat to one side.

"So you were out jogging when your wife was killed?" asked Ramesh Uppal gently.

"Yes, it's my morning routine," replied Gulshan Mehta. "I usually run with my friend Raghu Narang. We meet up at Leisure Valley Park, which is just across the road, at 6.30 am, and jog for thirty minutes."

"You leave for office at 9 am?" Ramesh continued with his questioning.

"Yes. I work as HR Manager with Universal Systems & Processors. The office is at Udyog Vihar – only a ten minutes drive from here."

"Your wife was not working?"

"No. We were office colleagues when we met and decided to get married – but she left the job after our marriage a year ago. Our company – my company – has a policy of not employing spouses. She was looking for another job – and was taking care of the house until she found one. We shifted into this apartment just after our marriage – so there was a lot of settling in still to do…"

Avinash spoke: "Your wife called you on your cellphone on the morning she was killed?"

"Yes." Gulshan choked – and then continued. "She called me just as I reached the park – before I met Raghu. Sangeeta told me that two strange men were standing at the door. They said they were newspaper vendors. They wanted to know whether we wanted doorstep delivery of newspapers."

"What did you do?" asked Avinash.

"I told her to send them away, since I had not called any newspaper vendor for discussions."

"And when you returned from your jog, you found your wife dead," observed Ramesh softly.

Gulshan Mehta looked downcast and said nothing.

Avinash Sharma drew out a sheaf of papers from his jacket pocket and placed them on the table between Gulshan Mehta and himself. "These are the details of the calls made from your wife's cellphone on the morning she was killed," he observed.

Gulshan Mehta looked at the sheaf of papers with a puzzled expression.

"The phone call made from your wife's cellphone to your cellphone at 6.35 am is also recorded in these documents."

Gulshan Mehta nodded slightly.

"These papers also contain details of the *location* of your wife's phone instrument when the calls were made. The location details are automatically recorded by virtue of the mobile towers that are being used."

Gulshan Mehta's face went blank. It was not clear whether he realized where the discussion was heading.

Avinash Sharma continued: "These papers also contain details of the location of *your* phone instrument that morning."

This time Gulshan Mehta's mouth fell open.

"The mobile tower location records show that *both* phone instruments were at the *identical* location when the 6.35 am telephone call was made from your wife's phone to your phone, Mr. Mehta," said Avinash Sharma grimly. "You made a call to yourself from your wife's phone – immediately after killing her – to give yourself an alibi, didn't you – to establish that she was still alive when you had reached the park? The actual fact was that you killed her, made the phone call to yourself and *then* you went for your jog!"

Gulshan Mehta's face went white. He had clearly never ever expected this kind of revelation. However, a spark of defiance still remained inside him.

"Are you claiming that *I* killed my wife?" he exclaimed. "Then how do you explain the driving license found next to my wife's body? Doesn't it link my wife's murder with the earlier killings of a decade back?" asked Gulshan Mehta, breaking into a sweat.

Avinash looked surprised. "What driving license are you talking about?" he asked.

Gulshan Mehta looked like he had just been slapped. He realized now the trap he had walked himself into. He began shaking.

Avinash Sharma continued unperturbed. "You have just admitted, in front of witnesses" – he tilted his head in the direction of Jeevan Mathur (who now realized why he had been asked to accompany the police duo to this meeting) and Ramesh Uppal – "that you have knowledge about the driving license of the woman killed nine years ago being found next to your wife's body. How do you know this? The discovery of the driving license has *never* been announced!"

Gulshan Mehta said nothing. Sweat dripped from his forehead in rivulets.

"I will tell you how you know," continued Avinash Sharma remorselessly. "You know because it is *you* who placed the license next to your wife's body after killing her – to make it look like the act of the notorious serial killer!"

Gulshan Mehta had not quite thrown in the towel yet. "How – how would I have come into the possession of the – the license?" he stuttered.

Ramesh Uppal pulled out a bunch of computer printouts from his briefcase and handed them to Avinash Sharma, who then placed them on the table in front of Gulshan Mehta.

"These are printouts of old newspaper stories of the nine year old killing of Rajshree Mishra – which we discovered on the internet," said Avinash to Gulshan, who had already guessed this. "Some of the photographs featuring the murdered girl while she was still alive show a young man amongst the friends around her. His features are remarkably similar to yours..."

Gulshan Mehta's face crumpled – and he slumped in his chair with a defeated look...

"This discovery led us to investigate your past, Mr. Mehta," said Avinash Sharma. "You and Rajshree Mishra began your careers together and in the same organization, didn't you? You had an office romance with Rajshree, in the same manner you had a romance eight years later with your future wife? You killed Rajshree, didn't you, when you discoverea that she was pregnant and was insisting on marriage? And you killed your wife Geetanjali, Rajshree's old friend, when she discovered Rajshree's old driving license amongst your possessions and began asking uncomfortable questions?"

Gulshan Mehta held his head in his hands and began sobbing.

Taking Stock

"So, Gulshan Mehta killed two women in a span of nine years! Is he the serial killer of Gurgaon?" asked Commissioner of Gurgaon Police, Rajender Saxena.

"No, sir," replied Detective Superintendent Avinash Sharma. "Gulshan Mehta copied the known methods of the person calling himself – or herself – 'The Gurgaon Killer', who is alleged to have committed several murders in the late nineteen nineties. Gulshan did this in order to cover his own tracks and divert attention from himself."

"Well, he got away with the first murder for nine years – he may never have been caught if he had not succumbed to his killer instincts once again a decade later."

"Once a killer, always a killer, sir!" said Avinash Sharma firmly. "That's why a murderer – or even an attempted murderer – must always be caught. Such people will always be a grave danger to society if they remain at large..."

"Well...the serial killer of the nineties is still at large.

So also is the person who attempted to kill Deepika Khera in the metro!"

"Yes. The second person may, again, be trying to copy the serial killer's methods – including that of giving a prior warning or tipping off where the body will be found..."

"...or the attempted murderer may be the same serial killer now re-surfaced!"

Avinash smiled grimly and said: "At least it is now clear that the Astor Green condominium murder was not committed by the serial killer but by the husband – who imitated the serial killer's methods of sending a message indicating the location of the body and who also planted a link, in the form of the driving license, with a nine year old murder which was alleged to have been committed by the serial killer..."

"...But which was actually committed by Geetanjali Mehta's killer himself, nine years ago. That was a brilliant piece of investigative work, Avinash! My compliments to you."

"Thank you, sir. At least the press will now have to backtrack from serial killer theories. The panic will stop spreading."

"The panic with regard to the serial killer will not stop spreading until you solve the mystery of the attempted murder of Deepika Khera," observed Commissioner Saxena.

"I understand, sir. I will get on that job immediately. Also, sir, with your permission, I would like to re-open investigations into the five unsolved murders which were alleged to have been committed by the Gurgaon serial killer between the years 1994 and 2000. The 2001 murder of Rajshree Mishra has now been solved, with the arrest of Gulshan Mehta, but the other five still remain unsolved..."

"Go ahead. Of course, if there really was a serial killer – and if this person is still alive – then it is imperative that he – or she – is caught and put away. Such a menace cannot be allowed to roam free!"

"Very true sir – both investigations, the one on the Deepika Khera attempted murder and the one on the decade old murders, will proceed simultaneously."

"Wish you the best of luck – you will need it!"

The Picture Gets Confusing

Detective Inspector Raghuvir Prasad had retired from the Gurgaon police force two years ago. He lived with his wife and two married sons in the posh Sector 14 locality of old Gurgaon. He had, with great foresight, invested in two plots of land in this colony twenty years ago, when he was just forty two years of age, after selling off some ancestral property in his village in Jhajjar, south of Gurgaon.

A year before retirement, this rare breed of incorruptible government servant had sold off one of the plots at an astronomical price and had used up half the proceeds to build a modest house in the remaining plot of land.

The rest of the money was safely invested in fixed deposits and government bonds, thus enabling the retired police officer to live out a comfortable post retirement life with his wife, without any dependence on his sons – a luxury his meager pension would not have permitted.

Avinash Sharma and Ramesh Uppal visited the former police officer on the morning of the day after the arrest of Gulshan Mehta on two counts of murder.

Raghuvir Prasad served cups of steaming hot tea and *pakodas* to his guests and pointed to the newspapers spread on the dining table. "You are a famous man, Detective Avinash, sir."

"Please don't address me as 'sir'", responded Avinash Sharma. "Now that you are retired, you need not follow these official formalities." He took an appreciative sip of the tea and continued: "As for the fame – I was only doing my job. The hype will die down shortly!"

Raghuvir Prasad shook his head wisely. "The hype will continue – either positive or negative – as long as this serial killer frenzy continues," he observed.

"That is why we have come to you," said Avinash. "You were the investigating officer in the serial murder cases – all five of them. We need your help to nab the killer, if he – or she – is indeed the one who knifed Deepika Khera."

"He is the one," said former Detective Inspector Raghuvir Prasad firmly. "I am sure of it. The serial killer is back. And he is a man, not a woman…"

Jagdeesh Ruia, Chairman of Ruia Builders and Developers gripped the telephone receiver tightly and hissed into the mouthpiece: "What kind of a killer are you? You messed up such a simple job!"

The voice at the other end of the telephone connection snarled: "Don't bark at me you dog! Nobody talks to me like that and lives!"

Jagdeesh Ruia turned white. "Are you threatening me?"

"Learn to talk with respect – or you will be taught respect!"

Jagdeesh Ruia bit his lip to prevent the retort at the tip of his tongue from slipping out. It would not do to provoke the monster at the other end of the line.

Avinash Sharma and Ramesh Uppal stared in amazement at the retired Detective Inspector. "How can you be so sure that the serial killer is back – and that this same person tried to kill Deepika Khera?" Ramesh asked Raghuvir Prasad.

"I have, *literally*, lived with this murderer for seven years, right since 1994 when the first of the known killings was committed and I was appointed the investigating officer," stated Raghuvir. "Even though I never met the killer – much less caught him – I had studied his methods and patterns of behaviour so minutely that I began to feel as if I had known this person intimately since childhood!"

"You feel that the person who tried to kill Deepika Khera displayed the same personality traits as the serial killer of the past whose crimes you had been investigating?" Avinash hazarded a guess.

"Yes. So did the person who killed Geetanjali Mehta – exactly the same personality traits!"

Detective Inspector Ramesh Uppal almost dropped the cup of tea he was holding. "What are you saying, Raghuvir *ji*?" he asked in amazement. "Geetanjali Mehta's killer has been caught! It was her husband who killed her! Are you saying that Gulshan Mehta is the mysterious serial killer?"

"No. But the person who calls himself 'The Gurgaon Killer' was the mastermind behind Geetanjali Mehta's killing..."

Avinash Sharma took some time to digest this. When he finally spoke, he found it difficult to hide the skepticism in his voice. "Gulshan Mehta killed Rajshree Mishra, his earlier lover, in the same manner he killed his wife – with a knife slitting the throat – nine years ago. That has been established. Are you saying he did not do it?"

"Gulshan Mehta's hand may have done the actual deed on both occasions – nine years ago and now. But the serial killer was the mastermind behind both murders, of that I am sure! I am also more inclined to believe that, while Gulshan set up the stage for the murderous act, under the guidance of the serial killer, the actual deed of throat slitting on both occasions was probably done by the person calling himself 'The Gurgaon Killer'."

"How can you say that, Raghuvir *ji*?" asked Ramesh.

"Gulshan Mehta may have wanted to kill off his pregnant lover nine years ago," responded Raghuvir Prasad, "but how did he manage to carry out the killing so professionally? Gulshan was just about twenty one years old himself, fresh out of college – where did he learn to slit a throat so neatly and so professionally? Normally, such murders are done through strangulation – first -timers, especially men committing murder of women, find this the easiest method. This has been statistically proven. Yet, Gulshan managed to slit Rajshree's throat in a very professional and efficient manner, with minimum of blood letting. Even the most professional of killers would envy the manner in which the killing was carried out!"

"So, your surmise is that the serial killer helped Gulshan trap and kill Rajshree," said Ramesh Uppal slowly.

"Yes, I firmly believe this. In fact, a desperate Gulshan Mehta may have contacted dubious sources to hire a professional killer – to whom he could give a *supari* on Rajshree. The serial killer may have got to know of this and himself contacted Gulshan. The serial killer may be taking payments to commit killings – and why not? He – or she – satisfies the psychopathic urge to kill and gets paid for it also!"

"You think that the serial killer was paid by Gulshan to do away with Geetanjali also?" asked Ramesh.

"Yes! History repeated itself in the Geetanjali murder!"

"You are, of course, assuming that the mysterious serial killer of Gurgaon re-surfaced again after nine years to help Gulshan carry out his latest murder," observed Ramesh.

"The method and manner of the murder points in that direction," replied Raghuvir Prasad.

"But what makes you so convinced that this mysterious serial killer actually exists?" queried Ramesh, "The several murders you were investigating could actually have been committed by different persons!"

"My investigations clearly indicated that they were all the work of the same person. When I go into the details, you will understand."

"However, this mysterious serial killer always managed to stay a step or two ahead of you," commented Ramesh. "The killings continued, in spite of your investigations. You never did manage to capture the serial killer, did you?"

"I was close, my friend, very close – until, suddenly, the murderer disappeared. He vanished. The killings stopped. I began to think that the serial killer had died..."

"And now, equally suddenly, the killer has re-surfaced – or so you think," said Avinash Sharma.

"The person calling himself 'The Gurgaon Killer' has re-surfaced, Avinash *saab*," responded former Detective Inspector Raghuvir Prasad. "Unless you begin to understand this, many lives will be in danger..."

Death Uninterrupted

The police van carrying the prisoners from the Gurgaon district jail to the Gurgaon criminal courts came to a halt in the parking area of the judicial complex.

It was early morning. The crowds of litigants and their lawyers had not yet gathered in their full force. The courts would open only half-an-hour or so later. Still, the complex was filling up quickly – it would soon resemble a railway station at peak holiday season, except that the holiday cheer would be replaced by the grim and serious looks worn by litigants and lawyers the world over.

The van doors at the rear of the vehicle opened and several policemen jumped out. They were followed by several more men – shackled to each other by thick chains lashed around their arms. Once out of the vehicle, the prisoners were surrounded by policemen with rifles and roughly pushed towards the building. These men, criminals in the eyes of both law and society, had not just lost their freedom but their dignity as well.

Several of the shackled men were facing trial for cheating and fraud. Some were being prosecuted for robbery and attempts to murder. And one – Gulshan Mehta – was on trial for two murders.

Gulshan Mehta did not look well at all. He had evidently not been sleeping well; most first time prisoners did not sleep well during their initial few weeks in the rough environment of crowded jail cells. Some took longer to adjust. Some never did adjust.

Gulshan was unshaven and his eyes were bloodshot – probably with lack of sleep or with crying or both. He looked devastated at thought of where his fate and his deeds had brought him. He also looked extremely miserable in the company of his fellow shackled prisoners – and he had reason to be. Most of the men with him had long criminal backgrounds and looked it. Gulshan had been thrown into the company of the very dregs of society – and would probably remain in their company now for the rest of his life.

Unless the courts decided to hang him.

The group of armed policemen and their shackled prisoners entered the building and proceeded down the corridor towards the stairs that would take them to the prisoner holding area in the first floor. This is where the shackled men would remain for the rest of the working day as each was summoned for his respective hearing in separate courts.

The men would be relieved of their shackles while inside the holding area; they would be chained and handcuffed when taken to their respective hearings by their police escorts. They would be unchained again when they returned to the prisoner holding area.

The dividing line between humans and animals was well and truly obliterated when a person ended up as a captured criminal. The situation of a caged human was no better than a caged animal

– and in the case of those who had lived a reasonably well-off existence before they had ended up on the wrong side of the law, it was definitely a fate worse than death.

Gulshan Mehta was about to escape this fate worse than death.

The corridor – in fact the entire court complex – was quickly filling up with people. Some even brushed against the group of policemen and their shackled prisoners as they pushed their way down the corridor.

Then, with a sudden cry, Gulshan Mehta crumpled up and collapsed on the ground, dragging down with him two of the nearest shackled men.

The armed policemen quickly raised their rifles and formed a tight cordon around their prisoners. One of the policemen bent down over Gulshan Mehta and touched him.

When he raised his hand it was drenched in blood.

Pandemonium followed.

As the policemen forced the chained prisoners to lift up the profusely bleeding Gulshan Mehta and rush him back to the police van for transporting to the nearest hospital, the knife that had been thrust into his body got dislodged and fell to the ground. Screaming with fear, the men and women who had been standing nearby or had been just passing the group, begun running in all directions, further panicking the rest of the crowd.

A mini stampede followed, as prisoners, litigants and policemen alike rushed to flee from the spot when Gulshan Mehta had been knifed.

A killer was on the loose – and nobody wanted to hang around waiting to be the next recipient of a fatal knife stab.

Gulshan Mehta had been knifed in the heart. The mysterious perpetrator – certainly one of the people who had brushed against the group of policemen and chained prisoners in the corridor – had been an expert.

Gulshan died on the way to hospital.

The Aftermath

Detective Superintendent Avinash Sharma had just received a call. He listened and then switched off his mobile phone. His face was grim.

"Gulshan Mehta has been knifed to death," he announced to a shocked Detective Inspector Ramesh Uppal and retired Detective Inspector Raghuvir Prasad. "He was killed about fifteen minutes ago – right inside the criminal court complex!"

"The serial killer has silenced the one man who could have identified him!" said a grim Raghuvir Prasad.

Avinash Sharma jumped out of his seat. Ramesh Uppal followed. "It seems that you were right," said Avinash looking at Raghuvir Prasad. "The serial killer is back and was the mastermind behind the Astor Green Condominium murder. Gulshan Mehta was a tool."

"And the tool has been silenced to prevent him from spilling the beans and identifying his backer and guide!" exclaimed Ramesh.

"We need to rush to the site of the crime and then to the hospital where Gulshan's body is lying – but we'll be back," said Avinash quickly. "Now, more than ever, we need your help to nab this serial killer," he told Raghuvir Prasad.

"Come back by all means!" responded Raghuvir Prasad. "I have unfinished business with 'The Gurgaon Killer'. Let's work together to capture this menace..."

Jeevan Mathur's phone call came when Avinash Sharma and Ramesh Uppal were driving out of the Sector 14 residential area and heading towards the Gurgaon district courts complex. Ramesh was driving the official jeep and Avinash was sitting in the passenger seat. Avinash's two armed police escorts sat in the back of the jeep.

"Another e-mail has been received," announced Jeevan over the phone. "It may be a prank – or it may actually be from the serial killer."

"Does it talk of a killing in the district courts complex?" asked Avinash.

There was a pause at the other end of the phone connection.

"How did you know that?" asked a surprised Jeevan.

"The murder has already been committed – Gulshan Mehta was knifed to death around twenty-twenty five minutes ago in the court complex, while he was being taken for his remand hearing."

There was a shocked silence while Jeevan Mathur digested this piece of information.

"The e-mail was received just two-three minutes ago – I was working on the computer and saw it immediately," said Jeevan. "The e-mail *did* mention that the murder had already been committed. The killer must have sent the mail right *after* committing the murder – this person perhaps did not want a prior warning to backfire on him like it did in the case of the attempt on Deepika Khera."

Avinash drew a deep breath. "Then he – or she – must have used a computer not far from the court complex. That would explain the short time gap between the killing and the sending of the e-mail!"

"Unless the killer is not working alone," observed Jeevan Mathur.

Avinash grimaced. "Why are you trying to complicate my life?" he complained, as the jeep drove into the district courts complex. "Anyway, you may be right – but I will still follow up on this interesting lead; I will put police teams to scan the very recent visitors to all cyber cafes located near the court complex. We just might strike luck…"

Divyansh Malhotra put his hand on the shoulder of Lt. Col. (Retired) Amit Khera, Deepika's father, and said: "Don't worry, sir, Deepika is out of danger. We will ensure that Deepika gets the best medical attention possible. All expenses will be borne by the company – after all, your daughter was on official duty and carrying out official work when the incident occurred."

Lt. Col. Amit Khera gave a tired smile. "Thank you, Mr. Malhotra, for your kind words and equally kind gesture. I know Deepika is in safe hands. I'm yet to get over the shock of how close she was to death – but I know that everything will be all right in the end."

"I admire your spirit sir," responded Divyansh. He folded his hands in a *namaskar* in the direction of Deepika's mother and other relatives who had gathered at the hospital where Deepika was recovering. It would be several days before the Legal Manager of Malhotra Buildwell was well enough to move from the ICU into a private room and many more days before the eventual discharge.

However, the good news was that she was out of danger and well on the road to recovery.

Outside the building, as Divyansh Malhotra and Rani Suri stood at the entrance of Max Hospital in Gurgaon and waited for their car to be driven up from the parking area, they took stock of the situation.

"I hope the police soon catches the bastard who tried to kill Deepika!" said Rani vehemently.

"It appears to have been the work of the serial killer who is said to be at large. That's what the press alleges," responded Divyansh.

"I would have thought that the knifing was the work of a robber who had his eyes on Deepika's briefcase. He probably didn't realize that it was handcuffed to her wrist and panicked when he did. That would explain the botched knifing – it was done in a hurry, thank God! That's what saved Deepika."

"What you're saying sounds logical," observed Divyansh as they boarded the Mercedes that had been driven up to where they were standing by his chauffeur. "However, the e-mail warning sent to 'Gurgaon Window' is the trademark of the alleged serial killer. That's what led to the police team's presence in the train – and the ambulances at the stations. The killing was pre-planned."

"But why?"

"How does one know how a serial killer chooses his victims?"

"But this is scary – it could be just about anybody next time!"

"That's why there's a severe panic spreading in Gurgaon," observed Divyansh thoughtfully. "There may be a pattern in the way the victims are selected – but nobody knows what that is!"

Rani also looked thoughtful. "The attempt on Deepika could also have been made to *look* like it was the work of the serial killer – all that the 'copy cat' killer needed was to send an e-mail warning to the 'Gurgaon Window' mail address. After all, The Astor Court Condominium victim was actually killed by her husband, who sent the e-mail replicating the method of the serial killer..."

Divyansh and Rani of course did not know of the recent developments at the Gurgaon district courts complex that had taken place just about an hour ago.

Rani Suri continued with her chain of thought: "Could the murder attempt on Deepika, perhaps, have actually been the work of a business rival?" she asked. "After all, Deepika was carrying important papers in her briefcase. The Karmayogi Housing Society deal has got delayed because of this incident!"

"The thought did cross my mind," responded Divyansh. "There are several other developers who would have given their left arm to have grabbed the Karmayogi Housing Society property. We got there first. However, somebody may be trying to derail the deal – or delay it – so that time is gained to make a counter offer to the owners..."

"Would you like to share this thought with Detective Avinash?"

"I think I will..." said Divyansh, reaching for his phone.

The Suspect

Himanshu Dutt made his second visit of that day to the unimaginatively named Cyber World cyber café near the Gurgaon district courts complex.

His first visit had been at around 10.15 am, immediately after the internet café had opened for the day. Himanshu had departed immediately after sending out his two mails – noticing but not much caring about the uproar in the nearby district courts complex. He was always nervous of being followed and believed in constant movement. He would come back to the cyber café a little later to check his e-mail account to see if a response mail had come as a reaction to the one of the mails he had sent out.

So he returned after half-an-hour. He had found it difficult to wait any longer.

Returning to the Cyber World cyber cafe was probably the biggest mistake of his life.

His inbox did not contain any fresh unread mail. He decided to log out.

It was while Himanshu Dutt was logging out of his e-mail account that he noticed the grim looking policemen enter the internet café premises. There were two of them – and they were armed with machine guns.

He switched off the computer and tried to nonchalantly stroll over to the payment counter to pay his dues. He noticed the cyber café owner and the two policemen looking in his direction.

A cold hand gripped his heart.

Himanshu had been thoroughly trained to face such a situation – but the 'play acting' demos could never fully anticipate the tension and raw fear of the real situation.

Himanshu's legs were turning to jelly. He felt a strong urge to urinate.

He wanted to turn and run out of the shop. But that was a one way street to disaster and death. Those machine guns the two policemen were carrying would not be idle while he took to his feet and ran. They would burst into flames, as they were designed to do, and mercilessly smash bullet after bullet into his puny body.

Himanshu Dutt clearly had no option but to continue to walk to the payment counter.

As he reached the counter behind which sat the cyber café owner, one of the policemen stepped out of the shop and flipped open his cellphone. He began talking into the instrument, keeping his eyes focused on the entrance to the shop.

Himanshu paid his dues to the internet café owner, who studiously avoided looking at him. Mysterious. Very mysterious.

With an appearance of nonchalance that he certainly did not feel, Himanshu Dutt turned to leave the shop.

He noticed the policeman standing outside disconnect from a

call on his cellphone and look through the glass front of the cyber café at his colleague.

The policeman gave his head a tiny, very tiny, shake from the left to the right and back again.

Himanshu felt a great weight lift from his shoulders. He had been trained to notice such tiny body movements.

Whatever it was that the cops were planning – they would not nab him just yet.

He had gained some time…

As Himanshu Dutt left the cyber café and began walking towards the auto rickshaw stand nearby, he did not notice the grey Maruti Swift pull out from behind a parked car and begin following him slowly. Nor did he notice the motorcycle with two riders also pull out of a side road and begin following him.

Himanshu did not realise that he had become a very closely marked man…

Second Chance

Naresh Kumar, Director Operations at Ruia Builders and Developers (RBD) sat uncomfortably opposite his boss. On the other side of the massive desk, Jagdeesh Ruia, Chairman of RBD leaned back in his executive chair and commented: "So, the Karmayogi Housing Society deal has just got delayed, not derailed, by the murder attempt on the Malhotra Buildwell Legal Manager!"

"Yes, sir," responded Naresh Kumar. "The owners who have not yet signed the agreements are gathering again next week to do so."

Jagdeesh Ruia brooded. His sharp features were drawn into a deep frown. The sixty year old real estate mogul did not at all like the thought of his much younger upstart rival stealing the show from him like this.

"How do we get the deal killed?" he asked suddenly, his head jerking up.

Naresh Kumar looked perplexed. "I really don't know,

boss!" he answered truthfully. "Fifty of the sixty apartment owners have signed their sale agreements with Malhotra Buildwell. Ten apartment owners, five of whom live outside the city, have yet to sign. They had gathered here in Gurgaon – at the Karmayogi Housing Society complex, the day the Malhotra Buildwell Legal Manager got stabbed. She was carrying the sale agreements to the meeting. If the ten owners who have yet to sign their sale agreements – or even a few of them – do not sign, the block deal will not happen. That is part of the understanding. This clause is built into each agreement. If even one apartment owner does not sign, the deal falls through. Divyansh Malhotra needs the entire plot of land for his new mall – he needs to buy up the entire complex to be able to demolish it to make way for the new structure."

Jagdeesh Ruia's face became animated. "Do we know the names of the apartment owners who have not signed the sale agreements?"

"No. We have checked with a few property dealers but even they are not aware. No resident of Karmayogi Housing Society apartments is talking."

"The sale agreements that Deepika Khera was carrying when she was stabbed contained all the details," murmured Jagdeesh Ruia, half to himself. "A pity we could not lay our hands on them..."

Naresh Kumar froze. "I beg your pardon, sir? I do not understand..."

Jagdeesh Ruia smiled grimly. "The remaining ten sale agreements hold the clue to our success. If we can lay our hands on them, we will be able to get to know the details of the owners who are yet to sign. We can approach these owners with counter offers – better offers – and create a division amongst the apartment owners. If the signing of the agreements gets stalled, we can step in with our counter offer to the Malhotra Buildwell purchase price offer at a later date. This project can still be ours!"

Naresh Kumar thought carefully. He had not quite understood his Chairman's reference to the earlier missed opportunity regarding the ten sale agreements. At this moment, he did not want to travel down that road, though he knew that Jagdeesh Ruia's inadvertent comment would return to haunt him later. Right now, he had a challenge to address...

"The ten sale agreements will be in the custody of the Malhotra Buildwell Commercial Director Rani Suri," said Naresh Kumar. "She will carry them to the meeting with the apartment owners next week."

"We can't wait till the day of the meeting to lay our hands on the sale agreements," observed Jagdeesh Ruia with an edge in his voice. "We need to get our hands on the sale agreements as soon as possible. A glitch at the last moment – like last time – and our opportunity to stall the deal would be lost forever."

Naresh Kumar froze again. He simply could not understand the references his boss was going on making to the earlier lost opportunity. What earlier opportunity?

Jagdeesh Ruia continued with his observations: "We need to identify a mole in Rani Suri's office – a person who is close to her and who can be bought. We should do it today, itself." He looked at Naresh Kumar. "Get on the job, will you?"

Naresh Kumar simply nodded. He knew what had to be done. He had carried out such jobs for his employer before...

In Hot Pursuit

"We have two leads," observed Detective Superintendent Avinash Sharma. "One is a possible suspect and one is only a line of investigation..."

"The suspect is, of course, that young man who used the cyber café near the district courts immediately after Gulshan Mehta's stabbing," agreed Detective Inspector Ramesh Uppal. "What is the line of investigation that you are referring to?"

Avinash and Ramesh were sitting in the former's office sipping tea and taking stock after an eventful morning.

"I am referring to the thought that Divyansh Malhotra has planted in my mind..."

"Who? The real estate developer? Deepika Khera's employer?"

"Yes."

"What is this idea he has given you?"

"The murder attempt on Deepika Khera may be the result of business rivalry. Deepika was carrying important papers in her briefcase that morning – papers related to a real estate project worth several hundred crore rupees. The attempted murderer may have been actually after the briefcase, which was handcuffed to her wrist."

"How would the killer have unlocked the handcuff after murdering Deepika?"

"The killer may not have known that the briefcase was handcuffed to Deepika's wrist. He – or she – may have hoped to grab and run off with the briefcase after quietly killing Deepika in the metro train…"

"So we are back to the suggestion of a 'copy cat' murder attempt – send an e-mail and use a knife and make the murder appear to be the handiwork of the alleged serial killer!" Ramesh looked questioningly at Avinash and commented: "I had thought that we had debunked that theory with Gulshan Mehta's killing of this morning and after hearing what Raghuvir Prasad had to tell us."

"All the suggestions, one way or the other, that have so far been offered, are pure speculation based on not a single shred of evidence. Our job is to pursue every possible rational probability and lead available to us until it is proved baseless – or until we uncover the truth and capture the criminal or criminals…"

"Understood, boss!"

"Good. Right now, we have a couple of teams tailing that young man who identified himself as Himanshu Dutt in the cyber café when he used it this morning. He used that cyber café near the district courts immediately after Gulshan Mehta's stabbing, when the e-mail was sent to 'Gurgaon Window'. We have yet to identify the source of the e-mail through our cyber analysts, so we don't know whether the e-mail originated from the same place, but we can't lose sight of our only possible suspect. This young man came back to the cyber café a little later, and was observed behaving suspiciously. He clearly got a jolt when he saw our policemen enter the premises – so he is suspect. Apparently, he is a regular visitor to the cyber café. Let's see if he leads us to 'The Gugaon Killer.'"

"Why can't the man Himanshu Dutt himself be 'The Gurgaon Killer'? Why didn't you let the policemen arrest him on the spot? Why did you let him go?"

Avinash Sharma smiled. "It was a simple process of deduction that made me decide that the man Himanshu Dutt is himself not 'The Gurgaon Killer'. From the reports of the men on the ground and the copy of the id proof – his license – that he had submitted at the cyber café, it is clear that this man is in his mid twenties. Too young to be the alleged Gurgaon serial killer. Nine years ago, when the last of the alleged serial killer murders took place, this man Himanshu would have been in his mid teens. Difficult to imagine a serial killer of that age. More importantly, he would have been a mere child when the earlier killings took place!"

Ramesh Uppal looked suitably chastised. "So you are assuming that this man Himanshu Dutt is some kind of accomplice – and will, hopfully, lead us to the serial killer."

"Let us hope – and pray – that this happens…"

The Snitch

The place that Himanshu Dutt led the policemen who were tailing him in the grey Maruti Swift and on the motorcycle to was a farmhouse just off Sohna Road, right after the village – now a small town – called Badshahpur.

Himanshu was, of course, unaware that he was being tailed.

The auto rickshaw took 30 minutes to cover the distance from the cyber café near the Gurgaon district courts complex to the farmhouse. Half of Sohna Road had to be traversed to reach Badshahpur. On crossing the village, Himanshu's auto rickshaw did not proceed the rest of the way to the famous Sohna hot springs tourist complex but turned left into a small side road and stopped ten minutes later in front of the imposing gates of a farmhouse.

Himanshu paid off the auto rickshaw driver and disappeared through the gates into the interiors of the farmhouse complex. A guard stood outside the closed gates. A safe distance away, the surveillance team of policemen parked their vehicles and established contact with Detective Superintendent Avinash Sharma.

The *Lifestyle* end of season sale was in progress. The anchor departmental store in the DLF City Centre Mall on M.G. Road (this stretch is more popularly known as Mall Road) was crowded with shoppers. The whole place wore a festive look.

The management of the store had decorated up the whole place for the fortnight long event. There were balloons and streamers everywhere – hanging from every possible vantage point. Sale offer and discount announcements in typical lyrical Haryanvi-accented English (the store was part of an international chain but the staff was locally recruited, after all) blared out of the public address system, competing in decibel strength with the punk rock music being belted out from the piped music speakers.

People – men, women and children alike – fell all over each other to pick up bargain buys of winter clothing items they would never wear in the summer and which would become too small or tight or moth eaten or out of fashion by the time the next winter season arrived.

Still they bought – and stood in long queues at the payment counters for long minutes to ensure and formalize their purchase of clothing and accessory items they would soon forget that they had acquired with such great enthusiasm.

The great Indian middle class was cash rich and riding the India growth story. They had disposable income to burn – never mind the beggars and children of construction workers hanging around outside on the pavements and at the street light intersections and at the entrance of the parking lots where their newly acquired cars, purchased on monthly EMIs, stood.

These avid shoppers were the people who were growing the Indian economy – they went about their business in the joyful knowledge of their own worth, to themselves and to their country.

They were enjoying themselves – entire families together – with no generation schism visible, which is all that mattered in the end, didn't it?

Naresh Kumar, Director Operations at Ruia Builders and Developers strode into the departmental store, unmindful of the crowds. He walked straight to the escalator, unmindful of the tantalizing discount offers flashing around him from placards and banners and all manner of communication vehicles.

The escalator carried him up two floors to the Café Coffee Day hangout area.

Deepak Chaurasia was already sitting at a table, a half empty cup of cappuccino in front of him. Naresh Kumar joined him at the table without a word.

Deepak Chaurasia worked for Malhotra Buildwell. He worked in the Commercial Department, reporting to the Legal Manager (presently recovering from a knife wound in Max Hospital, Gurgaon) who, in turn, reported to the Commercial Director, the formidable Rani Suri.

Deepak Chaurasia was the mole in Malhotra Buildwell, identified by Naresh Kumar and his team of experts, with long experience in the field of what was popularly known as industrial espionage but what the likes of Naresh Kumar and his boss Jagdeesh Ruia preferred to term as 'information gathering'.

Information gathered through moles came at a price. Naresh Kumar put his hand in his inside jacket pocket and drew out a fat packet. He placed it on the table.

Deepak Chaurasia picked up the packet and quickly put in

the right pocket of his leather jacket. Surprisingly, he did not examine the contents.

Naresh admired the young man's confidence that he would not be short charged. Not that the young man needed to worry – Naresh had personally counted out the crisp five hundred rupee notes and placed them inside the packet he had just handed over to Deepak.

Deepak then kept his side of the bargain – he withdrew from his left pocket the plastic counter with the number '5' engraved on it, which the security guard at the entrance to the store had handed to him in return for the black laptop bag he had deposited.

Bags were not allowed into departmental stores – which suited both Naresh Kumar and Deepak Chaurasia just fine.

Was there a danger that there would be no bag at the security counter – that Deepak Chaurasia would take the money and run in return for an empty shopping bag or some such joke?

It was a risk; but Naresh Kumar rarely took risks. One of his assistants had been stationed at the entrance to the *Lifestyle* store to keep a watch out for Deepak Chaurasia. He had observed the young man depositing the black laptop bag at the security desk, according to the pre-arranged plan, and collect the plastic counter as his receipt. When Naresh received the confirmatory call on his cellphone, he disembarked from his chauffeur driven car parked just outside the building and strode into the store.

There was, of course, the risk that the laptop bag could be empty. But he had tried to take that into consideration in his plans. Naresh would check the contents of the bag before leaving the store. His assistants stationed in the store would maintain a close watch on Deepak – and promptly surround him in case of a phone call from Naresh, if the bag was found to be empty. Naresh Kumar reached out and took the plastic counter offered by

Deepak Chaurasia. An amusing thought passed through Naresh's head at that moment. The plastic counter he was taking custody of had the potential to completely alter the character and future of a real estate project worth several hundred crore rupees.

Naresh did not wait any further. He was not at all eager to drink coffee or tea. Without any expression on his face he stood up and left the coffee shop.

Once downstairs, Naresh walked carefully to the security desk near the entrance/exit of the store and proffered his precious plastic counter. He was rewarded with a black laptop bag. Unmindful of the crowd around him he unzipped the bag and quickly peered inside.

A sheaf of stamp paper with closely typed letters stared back at him.

Eureka!

Naresh Kumar left the departmental store with his black laptop bag without a backward glance at the anxious shoppers inside.

The Consignment

The police surveillance team observed the delivery van draw up to the gates of the farmhouse that very afternoon.

The van had the words 'Pearl Computers' painted on both its sides.

Two men emerged through the gates of the farmhouse and spoke to the executive sitting next to the driver of the van. After an exchange of words, the van was allowed into the farmhouse complex and the gates were shut behind it. Only the guard remained outside.

The police surveillance team had noted down the registration number of the van from its number plate. It was a Gurgaon number. Avinash Sharma, on receiving the news, ordered an immediate computer trace on the van's number and ownership.

The trace took ten minutes. The van's ownership was established. The computerized records with the Gurgaon motor vehicle registration authorities revealed the owner to be one 'Pearl Computers Ltd.' operating from shop number 109, Galleria Market, DLF City IV.

The van was still inside the farmhouse when a police team was dispatched to the premises of Pearl Computers in Galleria Market.

The police surveillance team observed the van leave the farmhouse after about an hour. In the meantime, the police team that had been quizzing the owner and manager of Pearl Computers in Galleria Market learnt that the van had delivered a consignment of twenty laptop computers to the farmhouse.

The order for the laptops had been placed a month ago. The order had been sealed with a fifty percent advance payment. The payment had been made in cash.

The twenty laptops had been sourced from the company's warehouses. They had been lying ready for delivery to the customer for several days.

That morning, an e-mail had been received requesting for delivery of the twenty laptops at the farmhouse located off Sohna Road. The e-mail had been sent from the id: 'h.dutt@gmail.com'. The mail had been signed off by one Himanshu Dutt.

The cyber crime wing of the Gurgaon Police then swung into action. The mail was traced to the source. It had, indeed, originated from Cyber World cyber café located near the Gurgaon district courts complex.

In the meantime, the origin of the e-mail sent by 'tgk@rediffmail.com' to 'Gurgaon Window' announcing the killing in the Gurgaon district courts complex had also been traced. It had also originated from a cyber café not far from the district courts – but a different internet café altogether. Not from Cyber World.

The trail seemed to have gone cold – Himanshu Dutt had not been the sender of 'The Gurgaon Killer' e-mail. But why had he acted so nervous at the sight of the cops?

The answer, perhaps, lay in the fact that a *second* e-mail had also been sent out by 'h.dutt@gmail.com' from Cyber World cyber café that morning. The records provided by the e-mail service provider to the police revealed that the recipient address 'mustaque.hussain@gmail.com' was located in Karachi, Pakistan…

Master Stroke

Naresh Kumar sat opposite his boss Jagdeesh Ruia. From behind his massive desk, the Chairman of Ruia Builders and Developers watched with eager anticipation while Naresh Kumar unzipped the black laptop bag that he had brought back from his visit to the *Lifestyle* departmental store in DLF City Centre Mall.

Naresh drew out the sheaf of typed stamp papers from the laptop bag and handed the bunch to Jagdeesh Ruia, who began studying them. Then a frown appeared on the forehead of the real estate tycoon.

"I don't understand this," said Jagdeesh Ruia in a puzzled tone, which slowly became tinged with anger. He quickly read the second stamp paper, then the third. Finally, with a frenzied gesture, he picked up the bunch of documents and flung them across the desk at a startled Naresh Kumar.

"We've been fooled!" snarled Jagdeesh Ruia. "You stupid idiot – you've paid for and brought back *crap*!"

Shocked out of his mind not only by the revelation that the documents he had taken out from the laptop bag were not what they were meant to be but also by the violent reaction of his boss, Naresh Kumar quickly read through the sheaf of stamp papers lying in front of him.

And then he understood why the Chairman of Ruia Builders and Developers was mad with rage.

The ten neatly typed agreements pertained to the purchase of a consignment of generators for one of the Malhotra Buildwell construction sites. All ten were the same agreement replicated.

They had been duped.

Naresh Kumar made a vain attempt to rationalize. "May be... maybe Deepak Chaurasia put these wrong agreements into the bag by mistake," he stuttered out.

Jagdeesh Ruia's face was red with rage. "I don't think so! Nor did this bastard Deepak trick you in his individual capacity to extract money out of you! Divyansh and Rani are behind this trick!"

Naresh Kumar's mouth fell open.

Jagdeesh Ruia's voice had gone cold. "Read the last sheet!" he commanded.

Naresh Kumar located the last sheet and read it with a shaking hand. Then he understood.

Typed neatly on the stamp paper were the words:

'INDUSTRIAL ESPIONAGE IS BAD FOR HEALTH'

Naresh did not appreciate the sense of humour.

Jagdeesh Ruia was now beside himself with rage. "Do you realize what you have gone and done? You have got me implicated in the murder attempt on Deepika Khera!"

Naresh Kumar realized that. His face went white.

"Your bastard of a mole was no spy – but a shitting loyalist of Divyansh and Rani! He must have informed his bosses the moment he received feelers from our side. And they set up this trap to confirm their suspicions!"

Naresh Kumar had no words to say. He was shaking.

"Clearly Divyansh Malhotra and Rani Suri had guessed that Deepika Khera's attacker was actually after the bag containing the sale agreements – now they have confirmation!" fumed Jagdeesh Ruia, his face as dark as his thoughts.

Naresh Kumar's blood froze in his veins.

"I had thought that the attacker was the serial killer the media is talking about!" exclaimed Naresh Kumar in a shaking voice. His earlier suspicions were now getting confirmed – his boss appeared to have engineered the murderous attack on the Malhotra Buildwell Legal Manager.

Jagdeesh Ruia stopped talking. He gave a dark look at his Director Operations. His lips formed a thin line. After a pause, he said coldly: "Now that your attempt to clandestinely acquire the sale agreements of the Karmayogi Society project has become public knowledge, this is what everybody will conclude – that RBD was behind the attack on Deepika…"

"But is it true?"

Jagdeesh Ruia's response was biting: "Your immediate concern is your failed attempt to plant a reliable mole in the Malhotra Buildwell organization. You need to worry about the compromising position that you have put yourself in – and me also! Your worry should be whether Divyansh Malhotra will slap a police case against you!"

Naresh Kumar kept quiet. Then he slowly got to his feet.

"I'm sorry that I failed so badly – please accept my resignation. I will send in my formal – written – resignation in a few minutes." He turned and shuffled out of the room.

Jagdeesh Ruia looked at the retreating back of Naresh Kumar with a hint of speculation on his face. He thought for a short while. Then he reached for his phone...

Terror Strikes

Avinash Sharma ordered the doubling of the strength of the police surveillance team outside the farmhouse near Badshahpur village. The police watchers were to keep a safe distance and ensure that they were not spotted. They were to spread out. The vigil was to be around-the-clock.

Avinash Sharma also ordered a look out for all suppliers and service providers to the farmhouse. He needed to send in an infiltrator into the farmhouse. If the residents of the farmhouse used a catering service or a horticulture service, for example, he could send in one or two of his men disguised as the employees of such service provider.

Avinash also ordered a check on the ownership records at the registry – the findings were a revelation.

The owners of the farmhouse near Badshahpur village were three in number. All three lived abroad. One was a second generation Indian, born and brought up in London. His name was Salim Iqbal and he owned and managed a computer software development company. He had obtained from the Indian government a Non Resident Indian (NRI) status, with all its attendant privileges, including that of owning property in India, in partnership with others or on his own. The second owner was named Mohammed Amin. He was also a second generation Indian – and a NRI. Mohammed Amin lived in Houston, Texas and it was found, to the consternation of Avinash Sharma and his seniors and team members, that he was a world renowned expert in explosives.

The third owner of the farmhouse under investigation was named Mustaque Hussain. The same name had featured in the e-mail address to which a mail had been sent by the mysterious young man named Himanshu Dutt, on the morning Gulshan Mehta had been killed, from the Cyber World internet café near the Gurgaon district courts complex. This man, as per the records, lived in Dubai. His nationality could not be ascertained – the records were mysteriously silent on that aspect (had the registry clerks been paid off to keep that column blank?) but the e-mail records provided by the e-mail service provider had already established that the mail had been sent to Karachi in Pakistan – which is where it had been accessed.

Detective Inspector Ramesh Uppal did a Google search on the name Mustaque Hussain. He factored in Dubai and Karachi in his query – and hit pay dirt.

When he narrated his findings to Avinash Sharma, the latter felt compelled to seek an immediate appointment, that very evening, with his superior, Commissioner of Gurgaon Police, Rajender Saxena. Detective Superintendent Avinash Sharma took Detective Inspector Ramesh Uppal with him to the meeting.

"One of the three owners of the Badshahpur farmhouse which we have put under surveillance, bears the same name and the same

Dubai residential address as a member of the inner council of the Pakistani hard line militant group Jamat-ud-Dawa," Detective Inspector Ramesh Uppal told Rajender Saxena in the presence of Avinash Sharma.

"The Jamat-ud-Dawa calls itself a charity group, and has been helping out in the flood relief work in Pakistan," said Avinash Sharma, taking over from Ramesh Uppal. "However, the JuD is better known by its alias – and shares the same Karachi headquarters as its alias."

Commissioner of Gurgaon Police, Rajender Saxena looked very interested and very concerned, all at the same time. "What is the alias of Jamat-ud-Dawa?" he asked.

Ramesh Uppal responded: "Sir, the Jamat-ud-Dawa is better known as Lashkar-e-Tayyeba, the notorious hardline terrorist organization. The Lashkar-e-Tayyeba has been blamed by the Indian government for the 2008 Mumbai attacks. The Lashkar-e-Tayyeba has been banned by the UN and several western countries."

The 2008 Mumbai attacks were more than ten coordinated shooting and bombing attacks across Mumbai, India's largest city, by Islamic terrorists from Pakistan. The attacks, which drew widespread condemnation across the world, began on 26 November 2008 and lasted until 29 November, killing at least 173 people and wounding at least 308.

Rajender Saxena almost jumped out of his chair in horror. "The *Lashkar-e-Tayyeba* owns a farmhouse in Gurgaon? This is a very dangerous development!"

"Right now this is all conjecture, sir," remarked Avinash. "The only link the farmhouse has with Pakistani terrorist groups is the name and address details of one of its owners. We are guessing that this Mustaque Hussain is the same man who has close links with

Lashkar-e-Tayyeba. But there is no proof. However, surveillance of the farmhouse has been stepped up – and I am working on ways of infiltration into the farmhouse complex."

"Step carefully, but do it fast," advised Rajender Saxena. "We need to know of any funny stuff going on – if funny stuff is actually going on, that is." He paused, then continued: "But no jumping the gun and rushing in with a raid without sufficient cause, please. The media will pounce on any smell of police high handedness. We are under intense media scrutiny on this serial killer case as it is!"

"We have a problem, there," admitted Avinash Sharma. "The killing of Gulshan Mehta has closed a door to a possible source of information on the serial killer. It is clear now that the serial killer was the mastermind behind Gulshan's two killings, though which of the two – Gulshan or the serial killer – did the actual throat slitting, we do not know. The attack on Deepika Khera may not have been by the serial killer."

"How do you know this?" queried Rajender Saxena.

"The real estate developer Divyansh Malhotra has provided us strong evidence that implicates one of his business rivals, Ruia Builders and Developers, in making clandestine efforts to obtain some documents pertaining to an upcoming and lucrative project of his," said Avinash. "These documents were in the possession of Deepika Khera when she was attacked. A senior official of RBD tried to obtain those documents again – he was photographed bribing a Malhotra Buildwell executive to give him the same documents. The attack on Deepika could have been a part of the conspiracy to obtain those documents."

"The picture is getting quite confusing," complained Commissioner of Gurgaon Police, Rajender Saxena. "Does the serial killer of Gurgaon exist or not?"

"He does, sir. He was the mastermind behind the killings attributed to Gulshan Mehta – who acted under his guidance. Of that we are now reasonably sure," stated Avinash with conviction. "The Deepika Khera attack might have been a 'copy cat' plan – an attempt to deflect attention away from the real culprits. Whatever be the truth behind the attack on Deepika Khera, we will find out very shortly…we will question this RBD official named Naresh Kumar regarding his attempt to steal Malhotra Buildwell documents – the same papers Deepika Khera was carrying when she was attacked. Our questioning may lead us to the truth behind the attack on Deepika…"

"As I have already mentioned, step carefully but step fast," said Commissioner of Gurgaon Police, Rajender Saxena. "You have two hot potato cases in your hands. One – the serial killing – is already a national sensation. If there is anything suspicious going on in that farmhouse with possible Pakistani terrorist links, you will have another national sensation in the making. You, Avinash, will be in the media spotlight more than Shah Rukh Khan and Aamir Khan put together!"

Covering Tracks

The e-mail was seen only an hour after it had been sent.

Jeevan and Pooja Mathur had been busy the whole day supervising the circulation of the latest issue of 'Gurgaon Window' in the apartment complexes of new Gurgaon. They did not have the time to check the e-mail account of 'Gurgaon Window' the whole day – after the morning inspection which had led to the discovery of the mail informing of the Gurgaon district court complex killing.

The 'Gurgaon Window' team possessed standing approval for the circulation of their magazine from the societies and their office bearers of most of the condominiums. However, cash payment for the circulation still had to be made every time – and the security guards of each apartment complex had to be physically supplied the requisite quantities of the publications to insert in the individual letter boxes.

All this ensured optimum readership – to the great satisfaction of the advertisers – but was a back breaking and tiring and a labour intensive process.

Jeevan and Pooja Mathur operated their magazine business with the minimum of staff – two to be exact – and therefore had to be closely involved in practically every aspect of operations, right from advertisement collection, designing, content writing, printing and circulation.

Pooja was, therefore, able to check the day's e-mails only in the late evening.

The mail from TGK was lodged in the 'inbox'. The sender was 'tgk@gmail.com'. Pooja frowned slightly and did a quick check. Yes, the earlier mails had been sent by 'tgk@rediffmail.com'. This was a new e-mail id.

The subject line read: YOU WILL FIND THE BODY IN THE PARKING LOT OF LEISURE VALLEY. The mail had no content and no signature.

Pooja grabbed her phone.

Ramesh Uppal led the police team to the parking lot of Gurgaon's famous Leisure Valley park, which was located near the residential colony South City - 1 and HUDA City Centre Metro Station. Even though it was late evening, the parking lot was full of cars and two wheelers. The park was a favourite of Gurgaon's morning and evening walkers. The latter were out in full force.

The police team spread out all over the parking lot, checking each car but trying not to create an alarm and panic. It took sometime – there were almost a fifty or so cars parked in the two acre parking area – but they eventually discovered the body.

It was a man. A man in his middle fifties. His throat had been slit. The body was placed in the driver's seat of the Mitsubishi Lancer. The head was thrown back in the pose of a sleeping man. A scarf covered the slit throat and the dried blood.

The dead man's wallet was found in his jacket pocket. It had not been emptied. Robbery did not appear to be a motive – though no briefcase or bag was visible in the car, which was unlocked.

The dead man's license and credit cards, found in his wallet, identified him clearly. His name was Naresh Kumar. He lived in the upmarket Essel Towers apartment complex on M.G. Road.

Naresh Kumar's visiting cards were also found in his wallet. When alive, he used to work as Director Operations at Ruia Builders and Developers, the well known real estate company.

The telephone call to Jagadeesh Ruia was made in the middle of the night. The call did not wake up Jagdeesh Ruia because he was not sleeping. He was sitting hunched up in a sofa in his study – a glass of whisky in his hand. He was brooding. His family members could make out that Jagadeesh Ruia was deeply upset about something and they stayed clear of him.

The rough voice cut through the telephone connection like a knife. "How dare you compromise me like this, you fool!"

"Mind your tongue!" snarled Jagadeesh Ruia. "I did what I had to!"

"Your actions have brought me unnecessary attention," the voice at the other end snarled back. "How dare you try to put the killing of your stupid henchman Naresh Kumar on my head!"

"I do not have to explain anything to you!" shouted Jagdeesh Ruia. "But it should be obvious to you that Naresh was about to be implicated in a case of attempting to steal documents from Malhotra Build well. When questioned, he would have dragged me into the mess."

"And now, by copying the TGK method, you think that you have deflected attention from yourself?"

"Of course!"

"Then you're a bigger fool than I had thought!'

Jagdeesh Ruia almost had a fit.

The voice at the other end continued remorselessly: "Why did you ask Naresh to steal the agreements in the first place? Can't you accept a loss and back off?"

"The whole damn mess has been created because of your failure with Deepika Khera!" spat out Jagdeesh Ruia. "You botched up that easy job and ruined my chances of getting those agreements!"

"Don't cover up your mistakes by blaming me, you fool!" snarled back the now very angry voice at the other end of the telephone connection. "You insisted on the sending out of the usual e-mail – but *before* the act. That put the cops on to me before I had a chance to do a proper job." The voice at the other end paused slightly and then hissed: "Or were you to trying to get me caught – perhaps killed?"

Jagdeesh Ruia, in spite of his terrible anger at being spoken to so rudely and so roughly, now realized that, perhaps, he had gone too far. He was dealing with a monster, after all.

"Can we stop blaming each other and get on with the job of extricating ourselves from this mess?" he asked in as placating a manner as he could.

"The mess is of your creation and cannot be wished away," snarled back the voice at the other end. "Regardless of Naresh Kumar's death, you will still be questioned regarding the attempt to steal the Malhotra Buildwell sale agreements. Your position has been compromised further by the sudden murder of Naresh Kumar. The police are already talking of TGK 'copy cat' murders

– they already felt that the attempt on Deepika Khera was one such. You cannot escape suspicion and the consequent questioning by the police. What if you talk a bit too much? What if you talk about *me*?"

A cold hand clutched at Jagdeesh Ruia's heart. "I will take all legal recourse there is at my disposal. I will not be questioned," he said.

"Easier said than done! You have put me in danger!"

Jagdeesh Ruia broke out into a sweat. "Let us talk this out face-to-face tomorrow. We can think of some way out of this situation…nothing is impossible." He waited for a response. When none came, he continued: "I will leave Gurgaon tomorrow morning. I will not give the police a chance to meet me. I will drive to my farm in Manesar, while my lawyers tackle the police and prepare my responses to their possible questions. Naresh was acting alone in the matter of the Malhotra Buildwell documents. That will be my stand. I will get the PR department to issue out an appropriate press statement regarding Naresh Kumar's unauthorized clandestine activities – and my sorrow at his death."

A click of the phone connection being disconnected at the other end was the only sound that greeted him.

Infiltration

The discovery of the body of Naresh Kumar had taken place too late in the day to make it to the front pages of next morning's newspapers. The newspapers had already gone for printing, late in the evening, by the time the reporters got wind of the discovery of another possible victim of the alleged serial killer of Gurgaon.

The television and cable channels were not bound by such deadlines. The next morning's news broadcasts on all the channels were full of the murder. Earnest looking reporters were shown standing in the parking area of Gurgaon's Leisure Valley park, pointing to the spot where the Mitsubishi Lancer had stood when the body of Naresh Kumar was discovered inside it. Elderly morning walkers were quizzed on the screen about the security measures in the park. Most complained that security was inadequate. Some spoke darkly of undiscovered rapes and murders that had been committed in the park over the years.

The serial killer of Gurgaon was back in the limelight. The residence-cum-office of 'Gurgaon Window' was under siege. Reporters and television crew camped outside, demanding an opportunity to interview Jeevan and Pooja Mathur regarding the spate of e-mails they had been receiving from 'The Gurgaon Killer'.

Avinash Sharma had ordered a heavy deployment of police security outside the residence-cum-office of 'Gurgaon Window'. There was a tight cordon of police around the Mathur's humble abode. This police presence, together with the television and cable vans and the vehicles of the reporters, created an unprecedented traffic jam around the lanes and by-lanes of the block of houses surrounding the home of Jeevan and Pooja Mathur. The neighbours were not complaining, however. They were kept too busy giving interviews before cameras and to press reporters about how long they had known Jeevan and Pooja Mathur and what a nice and energetic young couple they were. The Mathur daughters also received favourable reviews as did the friendly and helpful nature of the entire family.

The media circus was operating on all four gears.

Inside their house, Jeevan and Pooja Mathur handled the endless telephone calls from advertisers with a mixture of fatigue and happiness. Their magazine 'Gurgaon Window' was in the news for all the wrong reasons – but their advertisers wanted to cash in. The available space in the next issue had long been booked. Additional pages would have to be added. The next issue of 'Gurgaon Window' would be a bumper one…

So who was complaining?

The police, for one. The Gurgaon police came in for adverse comments in all the media for its failure to nab the serial killer. The sensational Gulshan Mehta murder had been too soon followed by the Naresh Kumar killing. Things were getting out of hand. Panic was beginning to take hold of Gurgaon in a viselike grip – or so claimed the electronic and print media journalists (the late morning newspapers had now begun featuring the story – the print media had caught up with the electronic media) and there were demands for an immediate press briefing by the police authorities.

The pressure on the Gurgaon police to deliver some immediate and concrete results was now overwhelming.

Avinash Sharma and Ramesh Uppal started their day in Gurgaon police headquarters unmindful of the media reporters gathered outside. The television cameras focussed on the front façade of the police headquarters building – and the reporters, speaking into the lenses, wondered aloud what the next moves of the investigating authorities would be.

Inside the building, Avinash Sharma and Ramesh Uppal focussed on the twin tasks for the day – putting a spy into the Badshahpur farmhouse and getting hold of Jagdeesh Ruia for questioning.

There was only one regular delivery service to the Badshahpur farmhouse. The residents of the farmhouse did not go out looking for groceries and household supplies. These items were delivered to them at the farmhouse itself – based on orders placed over telephone.

The police surveillance team had noted, on the first day itself, the arrival of the delivery van from 'Superneeds' supermarket which was located in the Omaxe Plaza Mall off Sohna Road. Avinash Sharma's team had immediately contacted the owner, who had been sworn to secrecy. A new recruit joined the groceries delivery team. He was, this morning, sitting in the passenger seat of the delivery van of 'Superneeds' supermarket that was on its way to the Badshahpur farmhouse.

This new deliveryman was actually an extremely well trained police detective specializing in undercover and criminal gang infiltration activities. It was hoped that he would be able to see and observe enough inside the farmhouse, while ostensibly making the grocery and household articles deliveries, to be able to conclude whether suspicious activities were being carried out behind the gates – or that the premises were actually being occupied by law -abiding citizens with no dangerous intentions on their minds.

In the meantime, Detective Superintendent Avinash Sharma received news from the advance police party, led by Detective Inspector Ramesh Uppal, which had gone to the headquarters of Ruia Builders and Developers to question Jagdeesh Ruia about the complaint of Malhotra Buildwell regarding the attempt to steal classified documents – and also about Naresh Kumar's mysterious death – that the Chairman of RBD had left, early that morning, for his farmhouse in Manesar.

Avinash Sharma had been a police detective for two decades and well understood that the Chairman of RBD was attempting to avoid questioning. This was enough to put him into high gear. Avinash Sharma immediately put together a police party – and left for Manesar in a convoy of three police jeeps.

He would be ready for any eventuality.

There was no way that the departing police party could avoid being noticed by the newspaper and television representatives who were gathered in large numbers outside the Gurgaon police headquarters, waiting for anything remotely like a tit bit of information on the mysterious murders taking place in the Millennium City. Some vans and cars took off in hot pursuit.

It was clear to all that some drama could be unfolding shortly…

Dying Is More Painful Than Death

The original Manesar village was a sleepy hamlet of about a thousand dwellings on the Delhi-Jaipur highway (NH-8), but since the late nineteen nineties it had been transformed into a boom town with some of the top brands of the world like Alcatel-Lucent, Samsung and Baxter establishing their factories there.

It's proximity to India's political nerve center – New Delhi – had also led the central government to establish headquarters of some institutions of national importance at Manesar, like the National Security Guards (NSG) and its training center, the National Bomb Data Centre and the National Brain Research Centre.

With the recent upgradation of the NH-8 into a newly developed expressway, Manesar was barely a thirty minute drive from central Gurgaon city.

The convoy of police jeeps shaved off ten minutes from that time. They arrived at the gates of Jagdeesh Ruia's farmhouse in Manesar just twenty minutes after they had left Gurgaon Police headquarters.

Detective Avinash was a man in a hurry. He simply could not allow his only possible link with the alleged serial killer of Gurgaon to escape his clutches…

The farmhouse was heavily guarded, as befitting a very rich man. There were several security guards at the front gate, perhaps a few more than usual. The policemen in the jeep ahead of the one Avinash Sharma was travelling in, jumped out of the vehicle as soon as it drew up to the front gates of the farmhouse and approached the security guards.

There was an exchange of conversation as Avinash Sharma waited impatiently. The security guards became busy on the intercom in the security booth outside the gates. A few minutes later, the gates were thrown open and two men in business suits strode out. The policemen escorted them to Avinash's jeep.

"I need to see Mr. Jagdeesh Ruia in connection with an investigation," Avinash told them briefly. "His office informed us that he is here."

The two executives noted Detective Superintendent Avinash Sharma's uniform and badge, looked helplessly at each other and then took a decision. They were not going to risk getting on the wrong side of the law for the sake of any boss. They stepped aside and indicated to the security guards to allow the convoy of police jeeps to pass through.

The jeeps drove up the long driveway, passing past well manicured lawns and trimmed trees and bushes. The rich certainly enjoyed a very different kind of 'rural' experience than the average farmer, thought Avinash to himself…

The jeeps swept under the massive porch of the farmhouse that resembled more a mansion in a film set that a farm cottage. A bearded gentleman in a safari suit was waiting at the porch for the police party. He introduced himself to Avinash Sharma.

"I am Mr. Jagdeesh Ruia's personal secretary," announced the bearded gentleman, extending his hand in a gesture of handshake. "My name is Satinder Rastogi."

"Pleased to meet you, Mr. Rastogi," responded Avinash, ignoring the proffered hand. "Can you please take me to Mr. Ruia? I need to meet him urgently!"

"Certainly, Superintendent *saab*!" said Satinder Rastogi cordially, withdrawing his hand. If he was nervous at the sight of so many policemen, he made sure not to show it. "Please step into the house. I will inform Mr. Ruia of your arrival."

Avinash Sharma and two police escorts climbed up the few steps to the front door and then stepped into a huge reception room, closely followed by Satinder Rastogi. The remaining policemen stayed outside, keeping a watchful eye on their surroundings, their rifles ready for immediate use, if it became necessary.

The room Avinash Sharma and the two police escorts entered was lavishly furnished, with ornate chairs and sofas and heavy teakwood tables. Huge paintings adorned the walls and expensive rugs decorated the floor. It was a room that was designed to impress.

Avinash had neither the time nor the inclination to be impressed. He was in a hurry to meet the real estate tycoon who had left – or was it 'fled'? – Gurgaon in a hurry that very morning.

"Can you now, please, inform Mr. Ruia of our arrival?" Avinash Sharma asked Satinder Rastogi impatiently.

Jagdeesh Ruia's personal secretary noted the impatience and decided not to aggravate the senior police officer any further. "Yes, immediately!" he responded. "Please take a seat – I will be right back!" Satinder Rastogi disappeared into the interior of the house as Avinash Sharma sat down on a nearby sofa. His police escorts remained standing, guns at the ready.

Avinash Sharma's cellphone beeped. He checked the number. It was from 'Gurgaon Window'.

Jeevan Mathur was on the line. "Another e-mail has come from TGK!" he announced.

A feeling of dread gripped Avinash Sharma at the pit of his stomach. He jumped up.

"What!" he exclaimed loudly, startling his police escorts. "Does the e-mail talk of a body?"

"Yes".

"Where is the body located?"

"At a farmhouse in Manesar. Jagdeesh Ruia's farmhouse."

"I'll call you back shortly!" said Avinash Sharma quickly and disconnected the call. At that very moment, he heard shouting from inside the house. Then a white faced Satinder Rastogi rushed up to Avinash Sharma.

"Its-its Mr. - Mr. Ruia!" exclaimed the personal secretary.

"What about him?" almost shouted Avinash. "Is – is he *dead*?"

"Come and see!" Satinder Rastogi turned and almost ran into the interior of the house. Avinash Sharma and his two police escorts quickly followed.

They were led to a study. The room was in a shambles. There appeared to have taken place, inside the room, a very violent struggle. Heavy furniture was lying overturned. Lamp shades and vases and decorative items lay broken and strewn about on the floor. There was blood splashed every where – on the walls and on the floor and on furniture. But no body.

Avinash Sharma stood shocked – both at the sight of so much blood and evidence of violence and also at the absence of any dead or wounded body.

He turned, perplexed, to Satinder Rastogi, who was standing next to him shivering with fright and absolutely white in the face, and asked: "What happened here? Where is Mr. Jagdeesh Ruia?"

Satinder Rastogi's voice was shaking badly when he replied. "I – I don't know! I knocked on the door several times. There was no response. Since you had expressed an urgency, I – I took the liberty of entering this room without a response to my knock. And then I saw *this*…!" He spread his hands out in a shocked gesture.

By now, a couple of security guards and some servants had gathered in the room and stood staring in shocked silence. Avinash quickly turned to the two policemen with him, who were also standing in stunned wonder at the bizarre sight of overturned and smashed furniture and so much blood, and ordered. "Go, quickly! Initiate a search in the house and in the grounds. Alert the other policemen. Make a thorough search. The people who fought in this room will be either in the house or in the grounds – dead or alive!"

As he turned back to survey the devastated room, Avinash Sharma heard one of the servants mutter: "Who would have thought that the old man would have had so much blood in him!"

The Missing Body

"We found no body – dead or wounded – either inside the house or in the grounds," reported Avinash Sharma to Commissioner of Gurgaon Police, Rajender Saxena.

"Jagdeesh Ruia has simply vanished?" asked Rajender Saxena wonderingly.

"Apparently so, and after what seems like a violent struggle with an attacker!"

"Are you sure it wasn't a set up?"

"It could have been a set up. There are several possibilities. An e-mail alert regarding a dead body, as per the usual method of the alleged serial killer, was certainly sent to the inbox of 'Gurgaon Window'. This mail could have originated from the serial killer or a 'copy cat' or could have been arranged by Jagdeesh Ruia himself to camouflage his escape."

"Are the cyber crime experts checking out the source of this e-mail?"

"Yes. This one – and the earlier ones as well."

"Have the farmhouse servants and security guards been questioned?"

"Every one of them. They all claim ignorance of what happened in the room and where Jagdeesh Ruia has disappeared – alive or dead. If they had been taken into confidence by Jagdeesh Ruia, in case the disappearance was stage managed, they are all doing a pretty good job of covering up."

"Everybody cannot be a good liar!"

"That's right, sir! Hence it looks like that the servants and the security guards genuinely do not know of what happened in the room and the whereabouts of their boss!"

"What about the staff at the RBD headquarters? Do they know anything? Is there a cover up at that end?"

"They are being questioned – but no breakthrough so far..."

"We seem to have come to a dead end in the matter of the serial killer, until he – or she – makes another killing, I suppose."

"Jagdeesh Ruia was our only probable link to the serial killer if he – or she – exists. There are several possibilities regarding the murders." Avinash ticked off the possibilities with his fingers as he spelt them out. "One: Jagdeesh Ruia is the serial killer. Two: Jagdeesh Ruia is not the serial killer but he copied the serial killer's methods in dealing with Deepika Khera and Naresh Kumar. Three: Jagdeesh Ruia used the services of the serial killer in much the same manner as Gulshan Mehta did. Jagdeesh Ruia's motive was to get his hands on the Malhotra Buildwell sale agreements – for which he was ready to kill. The serial killer then killed or kidnapped Jagdeesh Ruia fearing that he would expose him. Four: It was the serial killer who attacked Deepika Khera and Naresh Kumar – and Jagdeesh Ruia had nothing to do with these incidents. He has vanished because he feared arrest in the matter of the attempt to steal the Malhotra Buildwell sale agreements through Naresh Kumar's bribing of Deepak Chaurasia. Jagdeesh Ruia stage managed his disappearance in a manner to show that he was attacked by the serial killer."

"And how and when will we know, which one of these various scenarios, is the correct one?"

"Frankly, sir, at this moment in time I am not clear how soon the correct picture will emerge," admitted Avinash Sharma. "I think I will have to work with former Detective Inspector Raghuvir Prasad to re-investigate the murders of a decade ago which were attributed to the serial killer. I hope some new clues will emerge from a fresh look."

"No harm in trying. That's the only hope you have at the moment," commented Rajender Saxena. "In the meantime, I will arrange for a 'look out' notice to be circulated at all the airports in case Jagdeesh Ruia is alive and has stage managed his disappearance. If alive, he may try and flee the country..."

Undercover Discoveries

The television and newspaper journalists who had pursued the police convey to Manesar of course came to know the identity of the quarry and his mysterious disappearance. A police party had stayed back at Jagdeesh Ruia's farmhouse to ensure that the evidence available in the premises was not tampered with – that the room of the apparent struggle was not disturbed. However, the security guards, executives and servants present in the farmhouse could hardly be forced to keep silent – they emerged from the gates into the outside world to bask in the glare of their one lifetime opportunity of fame. They gave television and radio sound bites and interviews to the reporters in the manner of seasoned celebrities.

The story of Jagdeesh Ruia's mysterious struggle with a mysterious attacker and the real estate tycoon's equally mysterious disappearance was soon featuring on all the major national television and cable channels. Some international TV channels had also, by now, picked up the sensational story of the serial killer of India's Millennium City. They, too, featured the Jagdeesh Ruia story. The overnight murder of the real estate tycoon's right hand man Naresh Kumar – and the discovery of the body as a consequence of the by now familiar e-mail alert – drove the media into a frenzy of speculation.

The pressure on the Gurgaon police to issue a statement outlining the progress on the case of the serial killer was mounting by the minute. It was clear that a press conference, however brief, would need to be organized very soon and a media briefing given. The public demand for this was rising. Political voices were beginning to join the chorus of voices asking for an update from the Gurgaon police.

The Commissioner of Gurgaon Police, Rajender Saxena and the investigating officer Detective Superintendent Avinash Sharma were both faced with a serious dilemma – they had no update to give beyond what was already known to the press and the public.

The serial killing investigation appeared to have come to a dead end.

Avinash hated to admit it, but what was now needed was, perhaps, another murder.

Things were, however, looking up on another front. The police infiltrator, Detective Sub-inspector Piyush Pandey, had returned from his visit to the mysterious Badshahpur farmhouse with interesting information.

"There are about fifteen men staying in the farmhouse – most of them only in their twenties," he reported to Avinash Sharma and Ramesh Uppal.

Avinash looked very interested at this piece of information. "What do these young men do?" he asked.

"I was in the farmhouse for only one hour, supervising the delivery of the groceries and other household items from the van to the kitchen and the store – and taking payment from a man who looked like an estate manager. So I couldn't see much. What I *did* notice through an open door in the main hallway was that the young men were sitting in what looked like a classroom with a laptop computer in front of each one of them and that there were two older men giving out what sounded like instructions."

Ramesh looked disappointed. "So the farmhouse is the venue of some kind of a computer institute!" he exclaimed.

"I can't really say that for sure…" responded Detective Sub-inspector Piyush Pandey thoughtfully.

"What do you mean?" asked Avinash Sharma intrigued.

"Well, the two older men in the so-called classroom – who I think were some kind of instructors – wore Arab head gear and shoulder holsters containing pistols!"

Avinash Sharma and Ramesh Uppal looked startled. "They let you see that?" asked Avinash amazed.

"Not really. In the middle of the deliveries, I excused myself to go to the toilet. What I actually did was pass close by the open door of the room where all the men were sitting with their laptops and quickly looked in while passing by. One of the older men was taking off his jacket – the shoulder holster and pistol thus came into sight. The other man had already taken off his jacket and had slung it over a chair. So I saw his gun also."

"You saw anything else interesting?" asked Avinash quite intrigued at this report.

"Well, one of the young men was distributing pen drives to his companions."

"What's so odd about that?" asked Ramesh Uppal.

"The young man who was distributing the pen drives dropped one by mistake. Everybody near him jumped back suddenly – almost as if they feared that the fallen pen drive would explode!"

"Did it?" asked Avinash, now getting extremely interested.

"No, I don't think so – but I had already passed by the room and I didn't turn back in case somebody got suspicious of my intentions."

Avinash Sharma and Ramesh Uppal stared at each other and both shared the same thoughts. Ramesh attempted to sum up what they had learnt: "The farmhouse apparently belongs to people who have connections with the *Lashkar-e-Tayyeba* terrorist organization. A couple of Arab carrying pistols in shoulder holsters are giving some kind of training to many young men inside the farmhouse. A pen drive falls to the ground and the men in the farmhouse behave as if a bomb is about to explode. And a young man from the farmhouse sends an e-mail to Karachi to a man with the same name as an inner council member of the *Lashkar-e-Tayyeba.*"

"While looking for the serial killer we appear to have stumbled upon some dangerous terrorist activity at a planning stage!" exclaimed Detective Superintendent Avinash Sharma. "We will have to double the size of the surveillance team – and get the Intelligence Agencies involved!"

Going Places

Detective Superintendent Avinash Sharma and his team did not have to wait for too long for the mysterious men occupying the Badshahpur farmhouse to make their move.

In fact, the report of Detective Sub-Inspector Piyush Pandey, made after his undercover visit inside the farmhouse, had been filed just in time – Avinash Sharma was able to increase the size of the police surveillance team stationed outside the farmhouse to a sufficient enough size and strength in time to track what happened next.

Commissioner of Gurgaon Police, Rajender Saxena, had been alerted by Avinash Sharma about what Piyush Pandey had managed to observe inside the Badshahpur farmhouse during the one hour or so that he had been delivering goods as a disguised supermarket delivery executive. Rajender Saxena had immediately contacted the Union Home Ministry and had briefed key officials of the Indian Intelligence Services.

As it turned out, events moved much faster than anybody had expected. The officials of the Indian Intelligence Services were still busy discussing the implications of the discovery that had been made by the Gurgaon police at Badshahpur when the young men suddenly emerged from the farmhouse in one large group – and it was left to Avinash Sharma to deal with the crisis as it unfolded.

It was five o'clock in the afternoon – several hours after the delivery van from the 'Superneeds' supermarket had left the farmhouse – when the gates of the complex once again opened. Fifteen young men riding fifteen motorcycles and each carrying a black laptop bag strapped to his shoulder emerged from the Badshahpur farmhouse that was under observation by the Gurgaon Police.

The police immediately swung into action. The police surveillance team had not been ordered to stop or arrest those who might emerge from the farmhouse. They had been ordered to follow such persons. So they followed.

The police team by now contained four jeeps and five motorcycles. Eight of these vehicles set off in pursuit of the fifteen motorcycle borne and helmeted young men, keeping a safe and, hopefully, unobservable distance. A small team of three policemen remained back to keep a watch on the farmhouse. They retained one of the jeeps. The leader of the team, a sub-Inspector sitting in one of the jeeps that was pursuing the motorcyclists, also called Avinash Sharma to update him and ask for reinforcements.

The fifteen motorcyclists did not race down the entire stretch of Sohna Road. They all turned right at Golf Course Extension Road and then, half way down the road, they turned left. They were racing down the road that led to the huge building that housed the HUDA City Metro Station.

Detective Avinash, Detective Inspector Ramesh Uppal and four jeep loads of policemen immediately left the Gurgaon Police Headquarters and headed for the HUDA City Metro Station. They hoped to catch up with the motorcyclists and their own police comrades somewhere near the metro station.

Avinash Sharma and his contingent did not have to worry for long about where they would meet up with the followed and the followers. All fifteen motorcyclists entered the parking area of the metro station, purchased individual parking tickets, parked their bikes, strapped their helmets to the bike handles – and proceeded to enter the building.

The police jeeps and motorcycles that had followed them from the Badshahpur farmhouse entered the metro station one by one, keeping a gap of a minute or two between each entry so as not to raise suspicion of a major police activity. Avinash Sharma and his team also entered the metro station parking area around this time, again in a staggered manner but quickly, so as not to lose their quarry.

Fortunately, no train had entered the platform by the time the first team of policemen reached there. All the fifteen young men were hanging around the platform, at different locations, mingling with the crowd of waiting passengers.

The young men were all carrying their individual laptop bags, hung from their shoulders. Whatever it was that the bags contained, laptops or otherwise, had cleared the security x-ray machines installed at the entrance of the metro station – located right next to the ticketing counters and the first stop after the purchase of tickets.

The young men did not purchase any ticket. All fifteen men were in possession of metro rail smart cards. They had unlimited travel entitlement – until the money deposited against the smart cards, whatever amount it was, ran out.

The young men had also not failed the security frisking test. So, were they on some kind of a harmless errand?

The policemen and their officers also mingled with the crowd and waited for the next train, keeping a careful eye on the young men.

Constantly talking on their cellphones, the policemen co-ordinated with their superiors and each marked out one young man for his personal surveillance – much in the same manner that footballers stalk their opponents in the football field, one-to-one.

In this case, there were enough cops to tackle and stalk the young men in teams of two – two policemen to each one of the motorcyclists, who had abandoned their bikes for some reason to travel by the metro.

In case the young men decided to split forces, none of them would be lost sight of – the quick co-ordination between all the policeman managed through cellphone by Avinash Sharma and Ramesh Uppal had ensured that.

A train pulled up at the platform – and all boarded the different compartments at different points – the followed and the followers as well as the other waiting passengers. The train doors shut and the silver compartments pulled smartly out of the station and proceeded in the direction of Delhi. Where would the young men get off? Would all fifteen of them travel the entire 45 kilometer stretch, south to north, of this metro line – called Line 2 – crossing all thirty four stations, all the way to Jahangirpuri in the extreme north of Delhi? Or would they disembark earlier? Would they disembark together or separately at separate stations?

Were the young men going innocently to a place of recreation to enjoy some kind of an office outing – with the huge contingent of policemen following them uselessly, entailing a tremendous waste of taxpayer money?

Detective Superintendent Avinash Sharma guessed instinctively that this large group of young men had not left the Badshahpur farmhouse on some innocent errand. After all, as per his findings, the farmhouse appeared to be owned by the infamous *Lashkar-e-Tayyeba* terrorist organization. Among its residents were Arabs who seemed to carry shoulder holsters and pistols as easily as they wore shirts. With such a background, the young men could not be up to any good…

The train quickly crossed the Haryana state border that separated Gurgaon from Delhi. Five of the young men disembarked at New Delhi's Qutub Minar Metro Station. They were immediately followed by their police stalkers. The remaining ten young men continued on their journey in the train, also followed by their police stalkers. Avinash and Ramesh also remained in the train as it resumed its journey.

Avinash Sharma stayed in contact with the police party that had disembarked at Qutub Minar Metro Station. The five young men who had got off the train there did not leave the platform. They were hanging around the platform. They were apparently waiting for the next train to arrive…

Now alarm bells began ringing in Avinash Sharma's head. This was not normal behaviour. Any kind of behaviour that did not conform to normal pattern, particularly that of a large group, was a sign of impending trouble. He made a series of quick calls from his cellphone, alerting his team in the different coaches of the metro train to maintain very close and very strict vigilance on the ten young men under their observation. They were to alert Avinash Sharma immediately at the slightest sign of trouble.

The police team at Qutub Minar Metro Station was cautioned not to lose sight of their prey under any circumstances.

Avinash Sharma was too involved in the minute-to-minute monitoring of the stalking activity of the fifteen men to find time to update his superior of the operation he was currently leading and co-ordinating. He had no precious seconds available to him to waste on making phone calls other than that which was required for the immediate task of ensuring that all fifteen young men were being closely monitored. Besides, he had to keep his phone free for receiving incoming calls from his men, who kept calling with updates on the status of the young men they were tailing.

Avinash Sharma received a phone call. The five young men who had disembarked at the Qutub Minar Metro Station had boarded the next train towards Delhi. This was definitely odd behaviour. Avinash Sharma gave a quick call to Commissioner of Gurgaon Police, Rajender Saxena and briefed him of the situation. When Rajender Saxena began asking too many questions, Avinash Sharma cut the connection on his superior with a quick apology. He needed to focus on the drama that was unfolding on the metro line.

At the Rajiv Chowk Metro Station, five of the young men got off the train. The men Avinash Sharma and Ramesh Uppal were tailing, along with two other policemen, continued the journey northwards in the same train, with three other young men – and the six policemen who were tailing them. So Avinash and Ramesh continued to remain in the train that they had been travelling in from HUDA City Centre Metro Station in Gurgaon.

Through the phone, Detective Superintendent Avinash Sharma got to know from his team members that two of the young men who had disembarked at Rajiv Chowk Metro Station had boarded the next train headed west, which was going in the direction of Karol Bagh / Kirti Nagar / Janak Puri. They were, of course, being closely followed by their police stalkers.

The other three men had boarded the train headed out east, in the direction of Mandi House and the colonies across the river Yamuna. One of the men had then almost immediately disembarked at Barakhamba Road Metro Station as per the two policemen who were tailing him, appeared to be waiting for the next train that would then take him in the same direction he had been going earlier.

Avinash Sharma's puzzlement and bewilderment at these strange movements was beginning to give him a slight headache. Just what exactly was going on? Were these fifteen young men out on an inspection tour of the Delhi Metro network?

As soon as this thought passed through his mind, a glimmer of understanding began to creep slowly into Avinash's mind – like a shamefaced dog that had gone on an unauthorized run and was now crawling back into its master's house.

Avinash looked at the back of the young man he was tailing. *Was it possible?*

Detective Superintendent Avinash Sharma's suspicions turned to near conviction when, at Kashmere Gate Metro Station, four of the five young men, including the one Detective Inspector Ramesh Uppal was tailing, disembarked. Avinash's young man stayed on in the train – and so did Avinash and one more policeman.

Ramesh Uppal briefed Avinash Sharma on the phone of the movements of the four men who had got off the train at the Kashmere Gate Metro Station. Two had boarded the next train heading east, towards Seelmapur and Shahdara. Three men, including the one Ramesh was following, boarded a train headed west, towards Tis Hazari and Inder Lok.

Avinash Sharma, with his new found understanding, surmised that the three men headed west would again split forces at Inder Lok junction. One or two would board a train going in the direction of Shivaji Park / Peera Garhi while the remaining man or men would proceed towards Keshav Puram / Pitam Pura.

By now, Avinash had got the shocked realization of what

operation was being undertaken by the fifteen young men who had left the Badshahpur farmhouse that afternoon in motorcycles and who had travelled so far into Delhi on several different metro trains – though they had all left Gurgaon in the same train.

Avinash Sharma now understood why the men in the so-called classroom in the farmhouse had jumped back and quaked with fear when, as per the report of the undercover police agent Sub-Inspector Piyush Pandey, a pen drive had fallen to the ground from the hand of one of the young men…

After the train had crossed the Vidhan Sabha Metro Station, the man Avinash Sharma was following sat down on a bench and unzipped his laptop bag. Avinash Sharma realized that the time of reckoning had arrived. He also guessed that the event had been planned to occur all across the Delhi Metro Rail network at around almost the same time – in a synchronized and choreographed dance of death and destruction that would resonate around not just Delhi and India but around the whole world. The plan was so simple and so smart that it was, in a way horrifyingly beautiful. And terrible…

As the young man pulled out the laptop computer from the unzipped bag, Detective Superintendent Avinash Sharma quickly made several phone calls – to Detective Inspector Ramesh Uppal and other policemen who were following their own marked men. They, in turn, phoned the remaining policemen in the team that had left Gurgaon from the HUDA Metro Station and gave the instructions to act, while Avinash pulled aside the policeman with him and very quickly explained what would happen next. He ignored his companion's shocked expression and headed towards the seated young man.

The policeman quickly followed him.

The young man had, by now, switched on the laptop computer and was calmly staring at the screen of the machine as it came to life. Then he slowly pulled out a pen drive from his pocket.

As he reached out to insert the pen drive into the port of the laptop computer, the young man suddenly found his wrist gripped in a viselike grip. Another hand grabbed his hair and jerked his head up with a painful wrench. As he opened his mouth to scream, a second pair of hands grabbed the laptop computer from (where else?) his lap and pulled the pen drive from his hand.

Then, a hammer like fist smashed straight into his face and, as blood spurted out from his mouth and his cut lips, sudden darkness engulfed him…

The Deadly Conspiracy

The press conference could not be conducted in the press briefing room of the Gurgaon Police Headquarters. It was too small.

The entire nation's news media – both press and television – as well as most of the media from the rest of the world, wanted to be present at the news briefing regarding the discovery of the terrorist plot and the capture of the terrorists.

Aware that much more than the usual number of journalists and television and cable crews would be present at this latest press briefing by the Gurgaon police, Commissioner of Gurgaon Police, Rajender Saxena commandeered the three hundred seater 11,000 sq. ft. auditorium of Epicentre, the convention centre located near HUDA City Centre metro station.The press representatives besieged the entire complex several hours before the press conference was scheduled to begin. The harried security guards and staff of the complex had a very tough time managing the crowd of vehicles and TV vans that suddenly descended on them. The Epicentre had never witnessed such crowds before.

The huge press contingent was no surprise – it was to be expected. There is nothing more compelling than a serial killer story combined with the news of a world class terrorist plot and an almost last minute prevention of planned death and destruction on a massive scale.

No media house, big or small, would want to miss out on such a story…

Commissioner of Gurgaon Police, Rajender Saxena occupied the centre of the head table. To his left sat a senior official from the Union Home Ministry of the Central Government named Mathew Verghese. He was representing the Indian Intelligence Services. To Rajender Saxena's right sat Detective Superintendent Avinash Sharma.

Commissioner of Gurgaon Police, Rajender Saxena raised his arms. He was holding a pen drive in each hand.

"These are the bombs that were to be used to blow up the metro trains!" he announced. "There were fifteen of them. Each pen drive was to be used to blow up one train. A total of fifteen metro trains were to be blown up, while they were travelling between stations, in a space of ten or fifteen minutes."

A stunned silence fell over the assembled gathering. Then the hall erupted. Dozens of flash bulbs lit up the already brightly lit up press conference venue. Cameramen went berserk trying to capture the Police Commissioner holding up the pen drives for all to see. TV cameras panned the head table and then focused on the respective TV and cable channel reporters for quick sound bites.

"The bombs have, of course been diffused," announced the Police Commissioner quite unnecessarily. Then Rajender Saxena turned to look at Avinash Sharma. "This is the man who saved many thousands of people from certain death!" he announced.

More pandemonium. As the TV cameramen and press photographers went about their job of capturing the face of the current hero, the reporters jostled each other and raised hands high in the air to attract attention to themselves and their questions.

Rajender Saxena raised his hands again (his arms would soon begin aching, Avinash thought to himself wryly) and said in a loud voice: "I suggest that we allow Detective Superintendent Avinash Sharma to tell the facts of the case in his own way. Once he is through, you may put forward your questions to seek clarifications where necessary."

The hall quietened down. To prevent the restlessness of the assembled reporters from again reappearing, Avinash began quickly:

"It was our investigations into the apparent serial killings that led us to the discovery of this terrorist plot," said Avinash Sharma.

The press reporters made a note of this startling statement – and waited for more.

"The e-mail to 'Gurgaon Window' from the person calling himself – or herself – 'TGK', which announced the death of Gulshan Mehta at the Gurgaon District Courts complex was sent out not very long after the murder," continued Avinash Sharma. "This led us to suspect that a cyber café not very far from the Gurgaon District Courts complex had been used. We sent police teams to check the registers of these cyber cafes for details of the visitors to their premises during the immediate aftermath of Gulshan Mehta's killing in the court complex corridor."

"Smart thinking," commented a journalist from a national daily.

"It was a long shot," responded Avinash. "After all, the killer of Gulshan Mehta could have been partnered by an accomplice who could have been sitting in front of a computer far away and have been alerted to send the e-mail by a phone call or sms from the killer. However, our job is to follow up on any lead or line of thinking, no matter how small or big be the chances of success."

"It's good you followed up on this particular line of thinking – it led you to the terrorists, didn't it!" commented a young girl representing a popular television channel.

"In this case it certainly helped in a big way!" agreed Avinash Sharma. He went on to explain the noting of the suspicious body language of the nervous young man in Cyber World cyber café – who was visiting for the second time that morning – and the police team following him to the Badshahpur farmhouse.

"Why did you not arrest him right then and there, at the cyber café itself?" asked another journalist.

"Arrest him on what grounds?" replied Avinash Sharma. "We couldn't arrest him because he looked nervous at the sight of policemen. That's a common enough phenomenon. And he was too young to have been involved in the alleged serial killings of more than a decade back. But we did have him followed in the hope that he would lead us to the killer."

Avinash drank from a glass of water and then continued: "As it turned out, the e-mail in question was sent out from another cyber café in the vicinity of the District Courts complex. But we could not trace the sender. There were no records of visitors – and the owner has been investigated and cleared of suspicion."

"So the serial killer is still at large!" commented a cable television reporter.

"He – or she – will not be at large for long," responded Avinash Sharma grimly. "But to get back to the terrorist activity, it turns out that we made our discovery in the nick of time. The laptops were delivered to the farmhouse on the same day we began our surveillance and the terrorists went to Delhi to carry out their deadly operation the very next afternoon."

"How did you guess that the pen drives were actually bombs?" asked a lady reporter.

Avinash Sharma described the courageous undercover infiltration of the farmhouse by Detective Sub-Inspector Piyush Pandey and what he had observed. Avinash then described the stalking of the fifteen young men across the Delhi metro rail network and the gradual understanding that they were spreading themselves out to ensure that they were present in as many different trains as possible and on as many different routes as possible when the time came to activate and plant the bombs.

A shudder of horror went through the assembled crowd of journalists and reporters and cameramen and reporters.

"The magnitude of the operation was mind-boggling," commented Commissioner of Gurgaon Police, Rajender Saxena. "Thousands of people would have been killed or injured when the bombs went off in the fifteen metro trains all across Delhi. The terrorists had timed their operation to ensure bomb activation at around peak office hour – when people were returning home after work. The train compartments were full with peak hour crowds."

Avinash Sharma put a laptop on the table. "The fifteen laptops that the terrorists were carrying were loaded with special software that would activate the bombs in the pen drives. This is one of those laptop machines." Cameras again swung into action. Avinash continued: "The terrorists were trained to programme the software in the laptops and activate the bombs and set a timer."

The intelligence officer Mathew Verghese now spoke. "The fifteen young men were not suicide bombers. They were to insert the pen drive into the port, activate the bomb with the software programming, set a timer for five minutes or so – and then walk out of the train at the next station leaving behind the activated bomb in the laptop bag. It was expected that nobody would notice the unattended bag in the crowded train, thinking that it belonged to some or the other passenger!"

Avinash Sharma took over. "In the background of what we had found out and observed and deduced, I quickly understood what was happening and alerted my team all across the Delhi metro rail network to move in and arrest the terrorists. As soon as I saw the terrorist who I was following take out the pen drive from a pocket and begin to insert it into the port of his laptop, I knew that a bomb activation was about to take place. So I moved in and made my arrest. All the other terrorists were arrested around the same time – before they could activate their bombs!"

Commissioner of Gurgaon Police, Rajender Saxena added: "The terrorist organization behind this plot – it appears to be the *Lashkar-e-Tayyeba* – tried to take advantage of an apparent loophole in the metro rail security system. While bags are screened through the x-ray machines at the entrances, the contents of peoples' pockets are not examined, except by a cursory metal detector scan by bored policemen. Not that such scans reveal much. Often or not, as was the case that day, this cursory metal detector scan also does not take place! The pen drive bombs sailed though the security process lodged safely in the pockets of the terrorists..."

There was a silence. Then one of the journalists of a leading television channel summed up what everybody else in the room was feeling: "It appears that the citizens of Delhi own a huge debt of gratitude to Detective Superintendent Avinash Sharma and his team of Gurgaon police officers and policemen..."

Death Comes Uninvited

The hand that gripped the newspaper turned white at the knuckles. The serial killer of Gurgaon had been removed from the front pages. In fact, the hysteria had vanished – even the inside pages of all newspapers did not find it necessary to feature news or views on the existence or possible next moves of the alleged serial killer of Gurgaon.

It was as if this monster had never existed.

All that the national and local dailies featured that day were reports about the terrorist plot to devastate the Delhi metro rail system and kill thousands. The news reports were full of the investigation and the capture of the plotters.

The newspaper was thrown down with a violent oath. It would need another murder to ensure that 'The Gurgaon Killer' returned from oblivion…

Detective Superintendent Avinash Sharma, Detective Inspector Ramesh Uppal and retired Detective Inspector

Raghuvir Prasad stood at the entrance of the large hall and surveyed the backs of the men, women and children sitting cross legged on the carpeted floor, their faces turned reverently to the small stage at the extreme end of the room.

The crowd numbered about two hundred or so. They had come to this place from all over Delhi and Gurgaon. There were some foreigners present also. The men, women and children all sat quietly, many with hands folded, and listened to the discourse of the thickly bearded, long haired and white robed man sitting on a throne like chair on the stage. The men sat on the left side of the hall. The women and children sat on the right side of the hall. Whether this segregation of the sexes had happened by default or had been enforced, Avinash Sharma was not quite sure.

The stage and the backdrop were heavily decorated with colourful flowers. Thick incense smoke wafted in the air, adding to the slightly surreal atmosphere.

Several young women, also attired in long white robes, adorned the stage behind the seated and bearded man. They looked suitably awed to be standing so near the physical presence of the great man. They stood with heads bowed and hands folded.

Avinash Sharma indicated to his companions to join the men on the floor. They made themselves as comfortable as they could in the back row.

"God is present inside all of us, but very few of us possess the divine understanding to appreciate this," said the godman on the stage, continuing his discourse, unmindful of the newest additions to his audience. "Each one of us has been touched by God, each one of us is special. Each one of us has the godlike capacity to do great things, good things. Each one of us has the capacity to change this world of ours for the better. What we lack is this understanding of our own godliness and our ability to rise above the mundane and routine of our present lives."

There was a murmur of appreciation from the congregation. Who wouldn't like being compared to God?

From somewhere behind the stage, a harmonium and a table swung into action. As the music picked up, the godman launched into a full throated *bhajan*.

"O Lord, touch me with your grace," sang the godman.

"O Lord, touch me with your grace," repeated the men, women and children in the hall. Avinash Sharma, Ramesh Uppal and Raghuvir Prasad did not join in the singing.

"Give me the knowledge of the cosmos, give me the wealth of your love," continued the godman.

"Give me the knowledge of the cosmos, give me the wealth of your love," repeated the congregation.

"May there always be goodness in my soul and purity in my thoughts," concluded the godman.

"May there always be goodness in my soul and purity in my thoughts," concluded his followers.

A deep silence followed. Everybody in the hall sat quietly for several minutes, eyes closed in peaceful meditation. Then, with a deep sigh, Swami Satyasivanand got to his feet, folded his hands in a *namaskar* to his audience and slowly walked out of the hall through a door on the right side of the stage, closely followed by the young women who had stood behind his throne like chair on the stage.

The swami met the police officers in an inner sanctum of the ashram.

Swami Satyasivanand sat on another throne like chair – quite similar to the one he had occupied in the hall a little while ago. He was surrounded by light incense smoke and, of course, the young women. The women stood alert, ready to provide whatever assistance the holy man might require.

Avinash, Ramesh and Raghuvir occupied chairs in front of the godman.

"What can I do for you gentlemen?" asked Swami Satyasivanand. "Did you come to listen to my discourse or have you some other purpose?"

Swami Satyasivanand looked around fifty or so years of age. His long hair and thick beard were jet black. Whether the colour was natural or aided by dye, his three guests could not be sure – but the face, or whatever could be seen of it through the thick beard, was unlined and looked peaceful.

"We *did* come to listen to your discourse, *swami ji*," replied Avinash Sharma not untruthfully. "However, we also had another purpose."

Swami Satyasivanand tilted his head in a gesture of query. "What is that other purpose?"

"We would like to ask you for some details of the murder of Ritu Choudhury, which took place in this ashram sixteen years ago."

Swami Satyasivanand closed his eyes. The young women surrounding him went pale with worry. Was their Lord feeling unwell?

The three policemen sat quietly, not knowing what to say or do.

After a pregnant pause, the godman raised his right hand and pressed his forehead, his eyes still closed. Avinash Sharma noticed that Swami Satyasivanand had two thumbs on his right hand. The additional thumb appeared to be a small extension which curved inwards towards the godman's main thumb.

Finally, Swami Satyasivanand opened his eyes. He looked

pained. "You suddenly brought back very painful memories," he said slowly. "That horrible event of so long ago still haunts me. Poor, poor Ritu, what a lovely soul she was. She did not deserve to die the way she did – she was so young, so beautiful, so pure…"

Detective Superintendent Avinash Sharma said gently: "Ritu Choudhury's killer has never been found. This person may have resurfaced, after all these years. We need as much information about Ritu's murder as we can gather – we may get some pointers to the killer from the information you give us. We are investigating some recent murders. We have reason to believe that the recent murders may have been committed by the same person who killed Ritu sixteen years ago."

Swami Satyasivanand looked interested. "Ritu's killer is still active? You have an idea who this person is?"

"Yes and no," replied Avinash Sharma. "The investigations are still at an early stage. We would like your help to re-live the earlier case – the information you provide us may help us solve the recent cases."

"But the investigations into Ritu's death were very detailed. All the information is already present in the police records," responded Swami Satyasivanand.

"You are right, *swami ji*," said former Detective Inspector Raghuvir Prasad. "I was the Investigating Officer then, if you remember. I was provided with detailed information by you and the other residents of this ashram. However, I got nowhere in my search for the killer. Looking back now, after all these years, may give you – and us – a fresh perspective. That is why we are here."

For some reason, the godman looked slightly taken aback for a moment – or was it simply Avinash's imagination? Swami Satyasivanand quickly regained his composure, however, and: "Yes, yes – I recognize you. And I understand what you are saying… go ahead and ask me your questions and let me see if I remember all the details you need."

Avinash Sharma indicated to Ramesh Uppal to begin making notes. "Let's start with the discovery of Ritu's body," he suggested.

"Alright," responded Swami Satyasivanand, his eyes assuming a faraway look. "It all started with the discovery of the unsigned and typed letter in the donation box which stated that a dead body would be found behind the bushes of the kitchen garden at the rear of the ashram building. The name typed at the bottom of the letter was 'The Gurgaon Killer'…"

The Price Of Birth Is Death

Rani Suri entered the dining room to discover her father surreptitiously biting into a chocolate biscuit.

On seeing his daughter, Rani's father, retired banker Harishchand Suri, quickly dropped the half-eaten biscuit on to the plate in front of him and took a sip from his cup of sugarless tea.

Rani did not know whether to laugh or be furious.

She reached out and picked up the plate with the half -eaten chocolate biscuit. "Neha!" she called out.

The maidservant appeared.

"Who gave this to papa?" Rani asked the maidservant.

Neha hung her head and kept quiet.

Rani stepped forward, grabbed the maidservant's right hand – and made her take hold of the plate with the biscuit. "Do you want to kill my father?" she asked the maidservant, firmly but not unkindly.

Neha continued to maintain her silence. When *memsahib* was in the right and she was in the wrong, there was no point in entering into a pointless argument. She did, however, look at her elderly *sahib*, Harishchand Suri, through the corner of her eye. The old man studiously looked away in the other direction.

"Look Neha," said Rani, this time with a firmness tinged with a little anger, "the doctor's instructions are very clear. Papa is not to eat *anything* that is sweet or contains fat or oil. He has a very bad heart condition – he has had one heart attack already – and he is on a very strict diet as per doctor's orders. Why cannot you follow this simple no sweet, no fat, no oil rule?"

Neha's eyes welled up with tears.

Harishchand Suri found his voice. "Now look what you've done, Rani. You've made the poor girl cry."

Rani Suri turned on her father. "And you are the one to be blamed for that! Why do you ask the maid for food items that you are not supposed to have?"

"All right, all right – I'm sorry!" exclaimed Harishchand Suri. "I had an uneasy night – couldn't sleep properly. So I thought that I'd cheat a little at breakfast this morning to revive my spirits!" He became busy with his newspaper and tea.

Rani Suri looked concerned. "Do you want me to call the doctor?" she asked her father. "Are you still feeling uneasy?"

"No, I'm not feeling unwell now. I think the bad night was just a temporary blip."

Rani turned to the maidservant with a warning look. "If you value papa's life, do not listen to him when he asks for food items that he is not supposed to have – you understand?"

Neha nodded her head silently and backed out of the dining room, still holding on to the plate with the half eaten chocolate biscuit on it.

Rani Suri picked up her cellphone and dialed Lt. Col. (Retired) Amit Khera, father of Deepika Khera. "How is Deepika feeling, sir?" she asked, when the retired colonel came on the line. She listened for a while and then smiled. "Good to know of her rapid recovery. She is a very tough girl, your daughter! I will drop in at the hospital sometime in the afternoon today!"

As Rani cut the connection, she heard a strangled sound behind her. She swung around – and saw her father slump forward in his chair. The cup of tea fell from her father's hand – and his head crashed down on the dining table…

The ride in the ambulance was a nightmare.

The hospital was but a short distance away, but her father's struggle for life beneath the oxygen mask made every second appear to be a millennium. The heart attack this time had been a massive one – emergency attention was immediately required if Harishchand Suri was to survive this one.

The tears welled down Rani Suri's cheeks as she mentally prayed: *"Hang in there papa – just hang in there! Everything will be alright!"*

Divyansh Malhotra was already waiting at the Vedanta Medicity Hospital Emergency reception area when the ambulance drew up. The stretcher was ready – as was the oxygen equipment and the other emergency paraphernalia. The attendants took over and rushed the semi-conscious and gasping patient to the ICU, leaving a sobbing Rani to be comforted by Divyansh Malhotra.

"Please save papa!" sobbed Rani to no one in particular. "Papa cannot die!"

Divyansh put his arms around Rani and held her tight…

At the ashram located in the hills through which cut the Gurgaon-Faridabad Road like a curling ribbon, Swami Satyasivanand continued with his recollections.

"As had been predicted by the anonymous note found in the donation box, we discovered the dead body behind the bushes of the kitchen garden at the rear of the ashram building. It was Ritu – her throat had been slit."

Behind Swami Satyasivanand's throne-like chair, one of the white robed young women began sobbing.

Swami Satyasivanand's face had once again acquired a pained look, but he continued. "Ritu had no enemies. She was a very sweet child – only nineteen years old when she was murdered." His voice choked slightly, then he continued: "Ritu had entered the ashram four years before her death. She was an orphan – her parents had been killed in a road accident a couple of years before. Some relatives of hers who were my *bhakts* requested that we take her in. Seeing her sweet nature, I was very happy to receive little Ritu into the ashram."

Former Detective Inspector Raghuvir Prasad now stirred. "There was some scandal associated with Ritu Choudhury, was there not, *Swami ji*?" he asked.

Swami Satyasivanand grimaced. His face momentarily took on a hard look. Then he relaxed. "Yes, you are right. Ritu gave birth to a boy six months before she died."

"Who was the father?" asked Ramesh Uppal.

"She never did reveal the father's name," replied the godman. "No amount of questioning by me or her relatives or by the other residents of the ashram got Ritu to reveal the name of the child's father."

"And then she was murdered soon after...," murmured Avinash Sharma. "Could the murder have had a sex angle?"

"That is one of the lines of investigation that I had followed then," commented former Detective Inspector Raghuvir Prasad. "But there was no clue to the identity of the child's father. Nobody had ever seen Ritu Choudhury fraternizing with any boy or man."

"According to the anonymous note found in the donation box, the murderer was, apparently, a person who called himself 'The Gurgaon Killer'," offered the godman, looking as if he found the whole conversation distasteful.

"Yes, but that line of investigation – that the murder had been committed by a serial killer who attacked people randomly and without reason – also did not lead me anywhere," responded Raghuvir Prasad.

"Where is Ritu's child now?" asked Avinash Sharma.

"The boy has grown up in this Ashram," replied Swami Satyasivanand. "Ritu's relatives did not want him. I decided to keep the child here in memory of sweet little Ritu. He has grown up to become a fine young man – in fact, he will be leaving for foreign shores next week to continue with his studies."

Avinash changed tracks. "Can we take a look at the spot where Ritu's body had been found?" he asked.

"Certainly," responded Swami Satyasivanand. "Sunita, here, will take you there." He indicated to one of the white robed young women. (Avinash was thankful that the godman had not assigned the task to the woman who was sobbing away in a corner.) "You will find that we have erected a small memorial on the spot where Ritu's body had been discovered. Her friends in the ashram had wanted this."

The three policemen and the young woman called Sunita were soon standing in front of the memorial located behind the kitchen garden of the ashram. It was a secluded spot, hidden from the surroundings by bushes and a few trees. The body of Ritu Choudhury could have lain there undiscovered for several days if the residents of the ashram had not been alerted by the anonymous note in the donation box.

As Swami Satyasivanand had informed the policemen, there was a small stone structure at the site – a two feet by two feet slab on which a temple like dome had been erected. The memorial had been a labour of love – the murdered girl appeared to have been popular with the then ashram residents and well liked.

Avinash, Ramesh and Raghuvir saw a boy of about sixteen or seventeen years of age kneeling in front of the memorial to Ritu Choudhury. The boy's eyes were shut and his hands were folded. He appeared to be praying.

Avinash Sharma turned away so as not to disturb the boy – and then suddenly swung around again to stare at the boy's hands. He blinked twice and then stared again – digesting this new development.

The sixteen or seventeen year old boy who was kneeling in front the one-and-a-half-decade old memorial to the murdered Ritu Choudhury had two thumbs on his right hand. The additional thumb appeared to be a small extension which curved inwards towards the boy's main thumb...

Death Is Serious Business

"I never did get to see Ritu Choudhury's baby when I was investigating the case sixteen years ago," said former Detective Inspector Raghuvir Prasad, as the police officers and their policemen escorts were driving back to Gurgaon from the ashram, through the winding Gurgaon-Faridabad Road, as it cut through the Aravali hills. "The baby was only about six months old at the time of his mother's murder."

"So you never got to know then that Ritu Choudhury's child had an additional thumb in his right hand in the same manner as Swami Satyasivanand has in his right hand," commented Detective Superintendent Avinash Sharma.

"No. If I had known then, the murder case would have assumed a different complexity altogether!" exclaimed Raghuvir Prasad.

"At least now we know!" said Ramesh Uppal. "That woman Sunita confirmed to us that the boy we saw praying at the memorial is Ritu Choudhury's son, Ravi Choudhury."

"Yes, but this could be a simple coincidence," responded Avinash Sharma. His two companions smirked and gave knowing looks to each other. "I know, I know!" continued Avinash. "Godmen are not above seducing their women followers. We have heard many such cases before. But still, it could be a coincidence. The two thumbs in the boy's and *swami ji's* hands do not conclusively prove that they are son and father..."

"Nor does this piece of information prove that Swami Satyasivanand killed Ritu Choudhury," contributed Ramesh.

"And there is certainly no way we can conclude that Swami Satyasivanand is the serial killer!" rounded off Avinash.

"We have to be very careful in even airing such thoughts," said Raghuvir Prasad. "Swami Satyasivanand is a very powerful godman. He has among his followers some very important and powerful people of the country. He is well connected. Loose talk about him could get us into serious trouble!"

The three men fell into a deep silence.

There were three police jeeps in the convoy. The three police officers were travelling in the middle jeep. The first and third jeeps carried their police bodyguards – after the exposure of the *Lashkar-e-Tayyeba* terrorist plot by Avinash Sharma and Ramesh Uppal, their superior, Commissioner of Gurgaon Police, Rajender Saxena, had insisted that the duo be surrounded by police bodyguards at all times. There was always a danger of a reprisal attack on the police officers by the *Lashkar-e-Tayyeba,* felt Rajender Saxena, and he had obtained special permission for the round-the-clock protection of Avinash Sharma and Ramesh Uppal.

Now, suddenly, two hands shot out from the leading jeep, one from the right and one from the left side of the vehicle, indicating the other two police jeeps to slow down and pull to the side.

All three police jeeps came to a quick standstill by the side of the road, as the rest of the traffic sped by.

All three policemen in the lead jeep, except the driver, jumped out of their vehicle and raced over to Avinash Sharma's jeep. One of the policemen pointed into the trees by the side of the road. "There's a car lying between the foliage!" he exclaimed. "We saw a man lying in the driver's seat. He appears to be unconscious..."

"Let's check it out!" ordered Avinash Sharma.

They cleared their way to the car. Sure enough, there was, indeed, a man lying in the driver's seat, head slumped forward.

One of the policemen reached out and straightened the man. Then he muttered a loud oath.

Almost simultaneously, Avinash Sharma's cellphone rang. It was Jeevan Mathur.

Before Avinash could say anything, Jeevan spoke through the telephone connection: "There has been another e-mail!"

The policeman who had straightened the body raised his hand. It was covered in blood. Fresh blood.

"The body is lying in a car somewhere in the Faridabad-Gurgaon Road," continued Jeevan Mathur over the phone.

Avinash kept holding the cellphone to his ear while he stepped forward and stared down at the body in the car. The neck had been slit wide open. Blood was everywhere. The blood was fresh – the deed had been done not very long ago.

"The e-mail has been signed by 'The Gurgaon Killer'," concluded Jeevan on the phone.

Detective Superintendent Avinash Sharma knew the face of the dead man. It was a well known face. The bulging eyeballs and gaping mouth could not change the fact that Avinash was looking at the face of the missing real estate tycoon, Jagdeesh Ruia.

Death Is Never Far Away

It was late evening when a doctor, accompanied by two nurses, came up to where Divyansh Malhotra and Rani Suri sat in the ground floor waiting area of the hospital that was allotted to the attendants of patients admitted in the ICU.

Rani's father Harishchand Suri was still in the cardiac ICU of Gurgaon's Vedanta Medicity Hospital. He was now declared to be out of danger but would still need several days of very closely monitored medical treatment. He was not likely to leave the cardiac ICU for several days.

The doctor introduced himself. "I am Dr. Manohar Khanna. I am a member of Dr. Ratnakar's team. Are you named Divyansh, sir?"

"Yes I am," replied Divyansh Malhotra, highly surprised.

"May I request you to come to the ICU? The patient is insisting on meeting you."

"Is papa conscious?" asked Rani Suri, her eyes red from crying.

"On and off. He is still under oxygen – and very weak. He should not be straining himself or speaking to any one. But whenever he is conscious, the patient is repeating his demand to talk to Divyansh."

"I'll go and talk to him," said Divyansh, giving Rani's hand a reassuring squeeze.

"I'll come too," said Rani, getting up from her seat.

"No ma'am," responded Dr. Manohar Khanna. "Right now the patient is too weak to see or talk to anyone. We are only requesting Mr. Divyansh to come for a few minutes so that your father stops his restless demand and relaxes. Too many visitors will put an unnecessary strain on the patient who is very weak just now."

"I understand," said Rani, sitting down again. "But why does he want to meet you, Divyansh?"

"I'll soon find out," replied the real estate tycoon.

He followed the doctor and the nurses to the cardiac ICU on the first floor of the hospital.

Harishchand Suri looked extremely frail under the gas mask. The oxygen was being fed from a pipe fitted into the wall behind his bed. The oxygen supply unit would be on the other side of the wall, guessed Divyansh. A drip bag filled with saline and glucose solution was hooked up by the bedside with its tube leading into Harishchand Suri's left arm. Additional tubes led from the back of his hands and from his arms into blood pressure monitoring and heart beat monitoring machines.

Harishchand Suri appeared to be sleeping when Divyansh approached his bed. Divyansh stood there patiently. After a while, Rani's father opened his eyes. He saw Divyansh and slowly motioned to the nurse who was also standing by the side of the bed to remove the gas mask.

The nurse did so. Divyansh lowered his left ear to catch Harishchand's words. What he heard caught him off balance.

"Do you love Rani?" whispered Harishchand Suri, his voice shaking with weakness.

"I-I have never thought on such lines," stammered out Divyansh, forgetting to keep his voice low. The nurse gave him a warning look.

"Tell me quickly – I may not have much time left," whispered Harishchand Suri. "Do you love Rani?"

Divyansh thought furiously. Did he love Rani? Now that he had been asked so bluntly, Divyansh forced himself to face the issue head on. Did he love Rani?

Of course he did! He had loved Rani ever since she had first joined his team twelve years ago. She was caring, sweet natured, intelligent – and had carried a spark that had immediately ignited something inside him.

But he had been married then. There was no question of being disloyal to his wife of seven years…

Then, nine years ago, the divorce had happened – just after he had been dragged to court in that criminal cheating case. It was Rani who had stood by his side then, a pillar of support. And his love for her had grown stronger. But he had not let their relationship go beyond a professional level…

Why? Because he did not know whether Rani had ever felt the same way about him. And he would never try to find out – he had been badly burnt once already.

Now, Rani's father was waiting for his answer. Rani's father knew that he had a very short time left on this planet. He might survive this, his second heart attack, but his health would never recover. His motives were clear – he wanted to settle Rani's life before he passed on...

"Yes, I love Rani," said Divyansh simply, whispering into the old man's ear.

Harishchand Suri shut his eyes for a while. The nurse stirred. She looked at Divyansh warningly – the patient had been tired out by this interaction. The time had come for Divyansh to leave. Divyansh understood.

Before Divyansh could step away from the bedside, however, Harishchand Suri opened his eyes again and parted his lips. Divyansh dropped his ear to catch the old man's words.

"Rani loves you," whispered Harishchand Suri.

Divyansh Malhotra's head swam. What was the old man saying?

"Rani has loved you ever since she met you. I have seen her pine for you for twelve long years. I cannot see her like this any longer..." Harishchand Suri's voice tailed away.

The nurse swung into action. Enough was enough. There was only so much medical science would tolerate. She indicated to Divyansh Malhotra that the interaction was over. He would have to leave.

Divyansh was only too willing to comply. His head was in a shambles – his emotions a tangled heap of anxiety, concern, confusion, disbelief and joy.

He made as if to step away when Harishchand Patel again stirred. Harishchand's eyes remained closed but he mumbled something. The nurse had put her ear to the old man's lips in an attempt to catch his words. As Harishchand Patel finally drifted off into sleep, the nurse looked up at Divyansh.

"What did he say?" asked Divyansh.

The nurse looked puzzled. She replied, "I think he said: *'So much of human life is lost in waiting...'*"

Detective Superintendent Avinash Sharma dropped the reports on his table and exclaimed: "The mails to 'Gurgaon Window' have been coming from two separate e-mail ids and the mails from one of the accounts has been traced to a cyber café near Jagdeesh Ruia's office!"

Detective Inspector Ramesh Uppal scratched his head in a gesture of confusion. "If Jagdeesh Ruia was the serial killer then did he kill himself also?"

Avinash Sharma gave Ramesh Uppal a withering look. "You saw the body yourself – could that deep slash in the throat have been self-inflicted?"

"No, most certainly not. Jagdeesh Ruia was definitely murdered. He also wore a shocked expression on his face – as if couldn't believe what was happening to him. Also, somebody *did* send that e-mail to 'Gurgaon Window' just after the murder of Jagdeesh Ruia – to inform of the location of the body, in the established style and manner of 'The Gurgaon Killer'. So, have there actually been *two* 'Gurgaon Killers' – one, Jagdeesh Ruia – and another, second, murderer, working separately?"

"That's what we have to piece together, Ramesh – and fast. Things have gone far enough – it's about time we began making some deductions!"

Ramesh said thoughtfully: "The e-mails pertaining to the murder of Geetanjali Mehta, Gulshan Mehta and Jagdeesh Ruia and the attempted murder of Deepika Khera were sent from the e-mail account 'tgk@rediffmail.com'. The e-mails pertaining to the murder of Naresh Kumar and the location of Jagdeesh Ruia's body in the Manesar farmhouse were sent from the e-mail account 'tgk@gmail.com'. Does this tell us something?"

"To my mind, yes," responded Avinash Sharma equally thoughtfully. "The mails from the second e-mail account which you mentioned originated from a cyber café located very near Jagdeesh Ruia's office building. That e-mail id – 'tgk@gmail.com' was the one from which we received news that Jagdeesh Ruia's body would be found in his Manesar farmhouse."

"Which turned out to be untrue," observed Ramesh Uppal. "There was no body – only lots of blood!"

"That's right – which leads me to believe that Jagdeesh Ruia set up that drama to stage a disappearance act, and blame the serial killer for it!"

"So Jagdeesh Ruia sent the e-mail – or arranged for the e-mail to be sent..."

"Looks very much like it. The e-mail was sent from a location near his office. It was sent in the morning of his disappearance, which must have been a sudden decision. Hence the mail was sent out from the nearest possible 'outside office' location that was available."

Ramesh looked at Avinash carefully and observed: "The only other e-mail sent out from that e-mail account – 'tgk@gmail.com' – was the mail informing of the location of Naresh Kumar's body. Does this mean that it was Jagdeesh Ruia who killed his own Director Operations?"

"It would appear so," responded Avinash Sharma.

"The motive?"

"That is clear. Naresh Kumar had compromised Jagdeesh Ruia and the company Ruia Builders and Developers Ltd. by his botched attempt to steal sensitive documents of Malhotra Buildwell. We were scheduled to question Naresh Kumar regarding this matter – Jagdeesh Ruia would have stood exposed. Hence, he killed Naresh Kumar – this is what I surmise," responded Avinash Sharma."

"And he made the murder appear to have been committed by the alleged serial killer, by sending that e-mail to 'Gurgaon Window'!"

"It would appear so!"

"But then the most obvious suspect in the murderous attempt on Deepika Khera would be Jagdeesh Ruia! He was the one who was desperately trying to get his hands on those Karmayogi Housing Society sale agreements she was carrying with her – that much we now know from Naresh Kumar's failed attempt to steal them later."

"Except for the fact that the e-mail to 'Gurgaon Window' was sent from the wrong e-mail account, 'tgk@rediffmail.com' and not 'tgk@gmail.com', even I would have presumed that Jagdeesh Ruia was behind that murder attempt on Deepika Khera and not the other alleged serial killer," said Avinash thoughtfully.

Ramesh Uppal scratched his head again, in his characteristic style when confused. "Unless Jagdeesh had hired the person calling himself 'The Gurgaon Killer' to do a job on Deepika Khera and steal the documents she was carrying..." he said hesitantly.

Detective Superintendent Avinash Sharma stared at his colleague. "You know, Ramesh, you may have hit the nail on the head!" he exclaimed. "These two killers may have been working together! That's why their names keep cropping up together after almost every incident. 'The Gurgaon Killer' worked with Gulshan Mehta on a couple of murders. He could have worked with Jagdeesh Ruia also!"

The two men stared at each other, their minds working furiously.

"Naresh Kumar may have found out about this connection – and become a serious danger to Jagdeesh Ruia," continued Avinash. "This could have been another reason for Jagdeesh Ruia to have killed him!"

"And Jagdeesh Ruia may have overstepped himself when he tried to frame Naresh Kumar's murder on 'The Gurgaon Killer'!

He may have annoyed the serial killer enough to attempt to flee from him!" surmised Ramesh Uppal.

"You mean, Jagdeesh Ruia stage managed his disappearance to fool the serial killer as much as to fool us!" concluded Avinash.

There was a silence as the two police officers pondered over all the pieces of the vexing puzzle they had attempted to put together into some semblance of a sensible whole.

"Where does all this deducing get us?" asked Ramesh to his superior.

"I don't know," grinned Avinash. "But no brain work and hard work should go waste. Let's do a check on Jagdeesh Ruia's background as far back as we can go. We may get a clue to the serial killer's identity form Jagdeesh Ruia's past..."

"And where does that put Swami Satyasivanand? For some time I had thought that we had found our killer!"

"Fathering an illegitimate child from a devotee does not make a godman a serial killer..."

"Even if the mother met an unnatural death soon after the birth?"

"Of course it looks suspicious, Ramesh! I'm not a fool! But Ritu Choudhury's murder does not automatically make Swami Satyasivanand her killer – just as two thumbs on both Ritu's son's right hand and the godman's right hand does not automatically make our holy man the father..."

"Of course not!" responded Ramesh Uppal, his toned laced with sarcasm.

"Don't mock me, young man. Let's get to work and start gathering some evidence to back our highly imaginative deductions. But I must admit – the trail, finally, appears to be getting warm..."

An Unexpected Attack

Divyansh Malhotra took a sip of coffee, placed his cup back on the saucer and stared uncomfortably at Rani Suri. "I assure you, that's all he said to me," he uttered.

Rani looked puzzled. "He asked you to assure me that he was feeling well?" she asked in a tone of amazement. "Why couldn't he tell me so himself?"

Divyansh searched his mind for an answer. "Perhaps your father didn't want to upset you by calling you to his bedside in the ICU..." he said lamely.

Rani did not look convinced. "I have seen him in hospital before – remember that this is his *second* heart attack, not his first!"

Divyansh Malhotra had not become a real estate tycoon without a reason. He summoned up his customer handling skills. "Well you *could* ask your father all this when he recovers completely and returns home. I really can't explain his reasons for doing things – he'd explain best, I guess."

Rani Suri was immediately contrite. She bit her lips. "I'm sorry," she said quickly. "It's just that I feel disappointed at not getting that chance to see him…" her voice trembled and tailed away.

Divyansh very slowly reached out over the coffee shop table and placed his hand on hers. Rani stiffened slightly and then slowly relaxed. Divyansh spoke: "Look Rani, you've been through a lot lately – first with the murderous attack on Deepika and now with your father's sudden heart attack. I want you to take a few weeks off from work and simply concentrate on taking care of your father. Help him to recover fully."

Rani slowly shook her head. She said: "Dad will recover – he is in good hands. We – I – will meet him everyday in the hospital after he is out of the ICU, twice or thrice a day at least. But I can't leave you to manage on your own. This Karmayogi Society deal is a very big milestone in your career. You need all the help and support you can get right now. Those remaining sale agreements seem to be attracting a lot of unnecessary attention – I will not be able to relax until I get them signed by the few remaining sellers."

"This is all beyond the call of duty, Rani. It's not necessary. Business will take care of itself. Deals will come and go. What's most important is your dad's complete recovery – take care of him and forget everything else for the time being!"

Rani pulled her hand away from Divyansh's light grasp in a sudden gesture. "I will manage both my priorities equally well," she said tightly. "You need not worry."

Divyansh Malhotra's heart suddenly went out to this brave woman. What a fool he had been all these years! He had been so blind! Rani's father had been so right – he, Divyansh Malhotra, real estate tycoon and the toast of the business world, had wasted almost half his life in waiting. The most precious gift he could ever have received in his life had been right by his side for twelve long years and he had been too blind, too stupid, too caught up in himself to have seen and appreciated this…

But did he, now, have the guts, the nerve, to correct the situation? Would he be able to pour out his heart to Rani?

Divyansh did not get much of a chance to further pursue this thought – Rani suddenly pulled back her chair and jumped to her feet. "Shit!" she exclaimed, shattering the magic moment, "I had promised Col. Khera that I would drop in at Max Hospital to meet Deepika! They must be waiting. I have to go!"

"It's all right, Rani," began Divyansh, "I'm sure they will understand why you couldn't make it -," then he broke off. Rani was already half way across the length of the Café Coffee Day outlet on the top floor of the City Centre Mall on Gurgaon's M.G. Road. He jumped to his feet and quickly followed her, throwing down a hundred rupee note on the table to cover the bill and the tip.

Divyansh caught up with Rani on the escalator on the way down. "Look Rani, I have something important to discuss with you and it can't wait," he said quickly. "I suggest that you leave your car in the parking lot of this mall and I will call my driver, who is just outside, and I will take you to Max Hospital in my car. That way, I will also get to meet Deepika and also get to talk to you during the drive to Max."

Rani shook her shoulders slightly and nodded. "Sounds good, Divyansh," she responded. "Let's do it."

The couple reached the ground floor of the City Centre Mall and quickly walked towards the main entrance. Divyansh took out his cellphone from his pocket and speed dialed his driver.

"Bring the car up to the front of the mall, right opposite the *Lifestyle* showroom," Divyansh instructed his driver. "Keep the car engine running – we will reach you immediately and get inside."

Divyansh and Rani stepped out into the late afternoon sunlight. The sun would be setting soon and there was a pleasant glow in the sky.

They stepped across the green lawn in front of the mall as they saw Divyansh's Mercedes pull up to the pavement and stop. The driver got out and pulled open the right side passenger door.

Divyansh and Rani quickly walked over the well kept grass and reached the pavement. As Divyansh paused in front of the car, Rani automatically stepped on to the road right behind the Mercedes and began walking to the other side of the car. The driver kept the passenger door open, waiting for her to reach him and enter the car.

Divyansh heard the roar of an engine. He swung his head to the right – and saw a helmeted motorcyclist racing towards Rani!

It took Divyansh but a shocked instance to realize that Rani was only a few seconds away from being hit by the speeding motorcycle.

Rani had reached the passenger door. Her back was facing the motorcycle that was bearing down on her. Divyansh opened his mouth to shout out a warning.

Divyansh Malhotra's driver had seen the motorcyclist bearing down on Rani and the car. He reacted. With one smooth movement Divyansh's driver pushed a startled Rani into the car, slammed shut the vehicle door and swung himself backwards and flung himself on to the bonnet of the Mercedes!

The motorcycle raced passed at top speed, barely missing hitting the right side of the car and the driver, who was now lying sprawled on the bonnet of the Mercedes.

Divyansh looked on helplessly on as the motorcycle disappeared – going too fast for him to note down the registration number.

Rani lay sprawled on the rear seat of the Mercedes, numbed. But not as numbed as was Divyansh, who was sure from what he had observed that the motorcyclist had *deliberately* raced towards Rani in an attempt to hit her…

The Common Connection

"It was a *deliberate* attempt to harm – perhaps kill – Rani!" said Divyansh Malhotra.

"Your observation is correct," responded Detective Superintendent Avinash Sharma grimly. "There was also an e-mail sent around that time warning of an incident in front of City Centre Mall!"

Divyansh was stunned. "What are you saying?" he exclaimed. "This attempt by the motorcyclist to hit Rani was a handiwork of the Gurgaon serial killer?"

"It very much appears to be so," responded Detective Inspector Ramesh Uppal. "The e-mail was sent to 'Gurgaon Window'. The e-mail was signed off by 'The Gurgaon Killer'. The mail was sent from the e-mail account 'tgk@rediffmail.com' as was the earlier mails from this alleged serial killer."

"The circumstantial evidence indicates the hand of the serial killer," concluded Avinash Sharma.

Divyansh held his head in his head. "But this is madness! If the serial killer is targeting Rani, she will always be unsafe, inside or outside her house. This madman seems to be unstoppable!"

The three men were sitting in the drawing room of Rani's house. Rani, herself, was lying in her bedroom, sedated and half asleep. Divyansh had insisted that she return to her house immediately after the incident on the road in front of the City Centre Mall and had summoned his personal physician to attend to her. Rani's state of shock was easily understood – she had been through a lot of stress in a very short period of time; the doctor had prescribed complete rest and had sedated her to facilitate this.

Divyansh had now begun to feel an anger welling up inside him that he had not known for nine years...

"When was this e-mail sent?" asked Divyansh. "How could the incident have been pre-planned? The decision to leave Rani's car in the basement parking of the City Centre Mall was taken just a few minutes before the incident...how could the serial killer have known that Rani would be getting into my car at that spot at that very moment?"

"The answer to your questions can be arrived at by a series of simple deductions, my friend," replied Avinash Sharma. "The serial killer is not working alone. He has a team. That we have understood by closely studying the murders he is alleged to have committed. The motorcyclist may or may not have been the serial killer himself – or herself." He paused and then looked pointedly at Divyansh. "The motorcyclist had clearly been following – stalking – either you or Rani, waiting for an opportunity to strike. As soon as this person on the motorcycle saw the chance to strike, he – or she – must have made a call to the mastermind or a gang member. And the e-mail was sent!"

"The e-mail was sent to the e-mail account of 'Gurgaon Window' at around the same time the attempt to harm Rani was being made," added Ramesh Uppal. "It was followed up by a sms to the cellphones of both Jeevan and Pooja Mathur – so they immediately checked out their magazine e-mail account. The sms trace had yielded nothing – a pre-paid sim card under a false name and address particulars."

Divyansh Malhotra turned pale. He was also seething with anger inside. "So this bastard – this serial killer – is now targeting either Rani or me or both!"

"And this killer had earlier targeted Deepika Khera, of your organization, also!" observed Ramesh Uppal.

"Then the bastard is none other than Jagdeesh Ruia!" exclaimed Divyansh, jumping to his feet. "You've already established the fact that he has been trying to get his hands on the Karmayogi Society sale agreements – to try and sabotage the project. That's why Jagdeesh disappeared – to escape your questioning. He is your man – the killer!"

"Jagdeesh Ruia is dead – his throat was slit. An e-mail was received informing of the location of the body at around the same time that we had discovered the body of Jagdeesh Ruia in his car." Avinash Sharma then gave Divyansh Malhotra a full update.

Divyansh sat down slowly, his mind a whirl of thoughts.

"Then Jagdeesh Ruia was not the person behind the attack on Deepika?" asked Divyansh.

"We think he was – but he was using the services of the killer, much like Gulshan Mehta used the services of the killer to get rid of his wife Geetanjali," responded Ramesh Uppal.

"But Gulshan had a decade old connection with the serial killer, according to your findings," pointed out Divyansh. "That's how they connected again after all these years..."

"Very true," observed Avinash. "We decided to delve into Jagdeesh Ruia's past also to see if we could dig out some clue to the identity of the killer who he appears to have been associating with now."

"Any luck?"

"We have one name – an old business partner who went to jail on a fraud charge that was made against both Jagdeesh Ruia and him but which was proved against only this person," said Avinash. Both Avinash and Ramesh looked at Divyansh. Then Avinash continued: "This person also has a past connection with you – which may explain a revenge motive..."

The Past Catches Up

Detective Superintendent Avinash Sharma and Detective Inspector Ramesh Uppal were back on the hilly Gurgaon-Faridabad Road. Sitting with Avinash in one jeep was Divyansh Malhotra. Ramesh was sitting with three police escorts in the jeep immediately behind theirs. A third jeep, loaded with police gunmen, followed at the rear of the three jeep convoy.

Avinash Sharma had arranged for a police team of three – including one policewoman – to provide round-the-clock security to Rani Suri. It was always possible that the unknown stalker could attempt to harm her again.

The convoy of police jeeps had just passed the spot on the side of the Gurgaon-Faridabad road where Jagdeesh Ruia's body had been found. Avinash had pointed out the spot to Divyansh as they had passed by.

The police jeeps were headed out to Faridabad – to the area known as Greenfields to be exact.

It was at Greenfields in Faridabad, very near to the tourist resort of Sohna, that Jagdeesh Ruia's old business partner had developed an affordable housing project ten years ago, after he had served out his jail term for fraud. He had not re-joined his partner Jagdeesh Ruia after his release from prison – but had struck out on his own.

It was to this old project site at Greenfields in Faridabad that the police party was headed.

This affordable housing project had been marketed, in good faith, by the real estate firm then owned by Divyansh Malhotra, a young, ambitious and upcoming property dealer of some repute. A young man in a hurry to make it big.

What Divyansh did not know then was that the project had been floated on deserted government land – the developer did not own even an inch of it. All he had to show was photocopies of fraudulently fabricated property registration deeds.

Then the fraud developer had eventually fled with Divyansh's clients' money, leaving the young property dealer to face the music.

Divyansh Malhota had got the last word. The cheat Rajeev Senapati had been finally caught, as a result of Divyansh Malhotra's dogged and desperate efforts.

Rajeev Senapati had been convicted and sent again, nine years back, to where he belonged. To jail.

Divyansh had won a pardon – he had been found to have been manipulated by the cheat Rajeev Senapati. It had still taken Divyansh many hard years of toil and stress to pay off the clients who had lost their life's savings to the cheat Rajeev Senapati.

It had been Divyansh Malhotra's greatest wish and prayer that Rajeev bloody Senapati would rot in – and die in – jail…

Now, according to what Avinash Sharma and Ramesh Uppal

had found, this cheat had completed his jail term and had been released from prison.

Had Rajeev Senapati come out of jail seeking revenge?

"The second murder attributed to the alleged serial took place in 1996," Avinash had explained to Divyansh when they had been discussing Jagdeesh Ruia's past connections in Rani Suri's house, before embarking on the drive to Faridabad. "The victim was the same man – a person who had been cheated in a property purchase matter – who had filed the fraud charges against Rajeev Senapati and Jagdeesh Ruia in 1995. Rajeev Senapati was in jail at the time of the murder. Jagdeesh Ruia was abroad – on a holiday in Singapore. So the obvious suspects were ruled out. Besides, the elements of the two year's earlier Ritu Choudhury murder were repeated – the anonymous note, the slit throat. So the myth of the serial killer began…

"Rajeev Senapati could have got the murder done through hired hoodlums or associates, even though he himself was in jail," Ramesh had observed. "He may have hit upon the idea of copying the elements of the unsolved Ritu Choudhury murder of 1994 to make the 1996 killing look like the work of a serial killer."

"The press had picked up the story of the common elements in both murders and went on to develop the hype on the alleged serial killer," commented Avinash Sharma.

"What are the chances that Rajeev Senapati could have had a hand in Ritu Choudhury's murder?" asked Divyansh Malhotra, shaking slightly with barely suppressed rage at the thought of the cheat he had sent to jail and who had caused him so much grief all those years ago.

"Looks very unlikely," responded Avinash Sharma. "Right now, it's Swami Satyasivanand who tops our list of suspects in the matter of the murder of Ritu Choudhury…"

"The godman?" Divyansh had been amazed. "What makes you think that?"

"We have our reasons," responded Avinash Sharma, giving Ramesh Uppal a warning look to keep quiet. "We can't reveal all our deductions and thinking until we have some concrete evidence to back up our thoughts. We could be sued for defamation of character. I shouldn't have mentioned our suspicions regarding Swami Satyasivanand to you. Do me a favour and keep quiet about this thought process, will you?"

"Of course!" said Divyansh. "Now coming back to the cheat Rajeev Senapati, how can we locate him? If this bastard is actually the person who is stalking Rani and me and trying to cause us harm out of a desire for revenge, then I will not be able to rest in peace until he is caught and put away behind bars. It will be difficult for Rani and me to live and work normally with this constant threat looming over our heads."

"I understand," Avinash had responded sympathetically. "We also need to track down this man Rajeev Senapati in order to question him with regard to his recent contacts, if any, with Jagdeesh Ruia. He may have been Jagdeesh Ruia's hatchet man in the Deepika Khera murder attempt, after all!"

"Our only clue to the potential whereabouts of Rajeev Senapati is the address mentioned in his jail records as his place of residence," said Ramesh Uppal. "It is in Greenfields, Faridabad."

Divyansh Malhotra's face had assumed a grim expression. "Greenfields is also the place where Rajeev Senapati had floated his fraudulent housing project – on government land."

"Then that's where we are next headed," Avinash had said, looking at Ramesh.

"Can I come, too?" Divyansh had asked. "I can lead you to

the project site and help you locate the address in Greenfields you are looking for. Besides, I would like to be present when you question the bastard Rajeev Senapati," Divyansh has said, still shaking with his anger. Rani Suri's close brush with death had shaken him badly.

"Come along, then," Avinash had said.

The route to Faridabad, cutting across the range of the Aravalli hills that separated Gurgaon from Faridabad, passed the imposing gates of the ashram of Swami Satyasivanand. On an impulse, Detective Superintendent Avinash Sharma halted the police convoy in front of the ashram gates.

"Do you remember that white robed woman standing near *swami ji* who began weeping when we started to talk about Ritu Choudhury's murder of sixteen years ago?" Avinash asked Detective Inspector Ramesh Uppal, who had jumped out of his jeep and come across to the vehicle of Avinash Sharma and Divyansh Malhotra to find out why they had stopped in front of the gates of Swami Satyasivanand's ashram.

Ramesh nodded.

"Well, I was thinking about that incident a little while ago and was wondering why this woman suddenly got so emotional when the topic of Ritu's murder came up," continued Avinash. "Had she been a close friend of Ritu? The woman looked to be in her middle thirties – the same age as Ritu Choudhury would have been had she been alive…"

"None of the other women in the room got upset or emotional when we started discussing the topic of Ritu Choudhury's murder with Swami Satyasivanand," commented Ramesh thoughtfully. "Yes, you may be right – this woman may have been a close friend of Ritu Choudhury's before the girl was murdered and she got emotional at the memory!"

Avinash Sharma looked meaningfully at Ramesh Uppal. "Then wouldn't it be a good idea to have a liitle chat with this woman?" he asked. "If she was close to Ritu, she may have got an inkling of the identity of her child's father."

"Raghuvir Prasad would surely have questioned all the close friends of Ritu Choudhury…"

"Some may have chosen not to speak then – they may decide to open up now. With time, compulsions and motivations do change."

"True." Ramesh stepped up to the guard box next to the ashram's imposing gates and spoke with the security men. The sudden stopping of the police jeeps at the gates had already been conveyed into the interiors of the ashram by the security guards at the gates. They had already received their instructions – the gates were swung open and the police convoy was allowed into the compound.

Swami Satyasivanand was not available. He was in meditation. The ashram manager met the police team. He was also bearded and white robed, but portly and short – the direct opposite of the lean and well built godman.

Avinash explained their mission. The ashram manager, Swami Prakashjyoti looked puzzled. "Unless you tell me the woman's name, I will not be able to identify her," he told Avinash Sharma and Ramesh Uppal, as Divyansh Malhotra looked on.

"I understand your problem…" began Avinash, when Ramesh quickly interrupted him. "The woman who took us to the memorial site of Ritu Choudhury – to the place where the poor girl's body was discovered sixteen years ago – I remember her name. She's called Sunita! Please call her. Sunita will identify the woman who was sobbing away when we were talking to Swami Satyasivanand ji."

Swami Prakashjyoti nodded slowly and spoke into the intercom.

After a short wait, Sunita appeared. She looked a bit nervous at the sight of the police officers.

Avinash explained what he wanted to know. Sunita looked at Swami Prakashjyoti. "Superintendent sir is referring to Taanya," she said quickly.

A sort of shadow passed across the eyes of Swami Prakashjyoti. After a short pause he said: "Ah Taanya, a very emotional woman! Yes, I do think she knew Ritu Choudhury all those years ago – Taanya also came to this ashram as a child and has been a resident here ever since. But I do not think that she and Ritu were very close friends."

"I think you can depend on us to find that out for ourselves, *swami ji*," responded Avinash Sharma, with a slight edge in his voice.

"Of course, of course!" hastily exclaimed Swami Prakashjyoti. "But, unfortunately, Taanya is not present in the ashram at the moment."

Avinash Sharma's voice became steely. "*Really*?" He looked coldly at Swami Prakashjyoti. "And *where* has Taanya suddenly disappeared to?"

"I-I'm not too sure," replied Swami Prakashjyoti wilting slightly in front of the hostile looks of the police officers. Avinash noticed that even the woman named Sunita was avoiding eye contact with anybody. There was also a slight bead of sweat on Sunita's forehead.

This was all getting very interesting indeed, thought Avinash to himself. From Ramesh's grim expression, Avinash could make out that his colleague's suspicions were also rising like a thermometer under a desert sun.

Detective Superintendent Avinash Sharma decided to back off a little. Too much aggression could backfire at this early stage of the investigation.

"Do you have an idea exactly when Taanya will be present again in the ashram?" asked Avinash as politely as he could.

"I-I'll have to check this out. I-I think she went out on an important errand. I think she would have gone to Delhi." Swami Prakashjyoti paused in a slightly flustered manner. "I think Taanya should be available sometime in the evening tomorrow. She should have returned to the ashram by then. Can I call you and inform you when she becomes available for a meeting with you, Detective *saab*?" he asked.

"I guess that's the best option at the moment," conceded Avinash. He turned to go – and then suddenly swung around. "Can we meet Ritu Choudhury's son? I think his name is Ravi..."

Swami Prakashjyoti began to look very unhappy. "He-he is also not present in the ashram right now..." his voice tailed off under the hard looks of Avinash Sharma and Ramesh Uppal.

"Really! Now what a coincidence!" Avinash Sharma's voice was all steel. "I suppose Ravi has also gone to Delhi with Taanya?"

"I-I th-think so!" exclaimed Swami Prakashjyoti, his forehead glistening with nervous sweat.

Avinash Sharma made up his mind. He knew what he had to do – as soon as he had exited the presence of this perspiring ashram manager, he would telephone police headquarters and put the ashram of Swami Satyasivanand under round the clock surveillance.

Surveillance had delivered rock solid results in the matter of the Badshahpur farmhouse. Avinash had a strong feeling that he would strike lucky again – but the police team had to be put in place around the ashram and outside the gates very quickly. The situation seemed to be developing into some kind of a climax at a very rapid pace, indeed.

The police officers and Divyansh Malhotra quickly made a quick exit from the ashram manager's presence and headed down the long and imposing corridor for the main door that led to the compound outside.

Suddenly, Divyansh stopped dead in his tracks.

Avinash turned to see what had disturbed the real estate tycoon. It was a large portrait of Swami Satyasivanand that was hung prominently on one wall. Divyansh was standing below it transfixed.

Avinash stepped up to the portrait and stared up at it, puzzled. It was a well crafted painting. The godman's features stood out prominently. The portrait painter had planted a peaceful smile on the serene face of Swami Satyasivanand. The portrait did succeed in its objective – of creating a feeling of reverence for Swami Satyasivanand in the mind of the viewer.

There was nothing reverential in the expression of Divyansh Malhotra as he gazed up at the painting. There was more shock and horror on Divyansh's face than reverence, thought Avinash Sharma.

"What's the matter?" asked Avinash. "Can we make a move, please? I need to take some urgent actions…I'd like to leave the ashram now. We will be back – you can check out the portraits and paintings later…"

Divyansh Malhotra turned to face Avinash Sharma. The detective took a quick look at the real estate tycoon's face – and realized that something momentous was about to happen. He was right.

When Divyansh was able to speak, his voice was hoarse. "Swami Satyasivanand's face bears an uncanny resemblance to the features of Rajeev Senapati!" blurted out Divyansh Malhotra. "Even though Swami Satyasivanand's face is covered by a thick beard, I can still make out. I cannot mistake that face ever!"

Avinash stared hard at Divyansh. He was momentarily speechless. Then he said: "Does Rajeev Senapati have a brother?"

"I don't know."

"Then let's find out if Swami Satyasivanand has a brother." Avinash turned quickly to Ramesh and said: "It's going to be a long night – we have a lot of research work to do. I do not think we will continue with our journey to Faridabad – it's very late in the evening anyway. Also, we now have more important work to do at police headquarters." Avinash turned back to Divyansh and asked: "*Now* what are you staring at?"

Divyansh was pointing a shaking finger at the hand of the godman as it had been portrayed in the painting. "Rajeev Senapati also has two thumbs on his right hand..." he said softly.

The Godman And The Conman

As the two police officers and the real estate tycoon and their police escorts hurried out of the ashram building and into the dark compound, which was insufficiently lit by only a couple of lamp posts, they were closely observed by a couple from a second floor window.

The late evening sky was pitch dark, but for the sparkle of a handful of stars. Yet the uniforms of the policemen glistened sufficiently menacingly as they strode across the compound and through the gates to the road outside where the jeeps were waiting.

The observing couple also noted from their second floor window the grim features of the ashram manager Swami Prakashjyoti standing on the porch of the main door and staring after the departing police party.

The couple in the second floor window also noted, as surely did Swami Prakashjyoti standing below, that only two of the three police jeeps departed in the direction of

Gurgaon. A police team and jeep had been left outside the gates of the ashram. No explanation had been given.

Ravi and Taanya backed off from the window and sat down on separate chairs. They had been asked by Swami Prakashjyoti not to move from this second floor room until further instructions. So they stayed put in the room. But Ravi was extremely puzzled by the two visits by the police party that he had witnessed in such a short span of time – and he was seeking answers.

"What is going on Taanya ji?" asked the almost seventeen year old to the woman who had been his mother's close friend before and immediately after he had been born.

Taanya avoided the boy's eyes and kept quiet for some time. Then she said softly: "There are things that are best not spoken about, ever..."

Ravi frowned. "What do you mean? Why are policemen coming to the ashram again and again? Why did they go to see my mother's memorial? Why were we asked to remain in this room while the police were inside the ashram?"

Taanya shut her eyes. She did not answer.

Ravi began to get agitated. "Why do you not answer, Taanya ji?" he asked. The boy turned his face in the direction of the window. "Why is that jeep full of policemen still standing outside the ashram gates?" he asked.

Taanya finally opened her eyes and responded: "Why are you getting so perturbed, Ravi? If there is a problem of some kind, the elders here will take care of it..."

Ravi frowned. "I am asking these questions because the policemen visited my mother's memorial during their earlier visit," he answered. "I think that their visit was made in connection with my mother's murder. I saw them – I was praying at the memorial when the policemen came to the site where my mother's body had been discovered. If the police have made some progress in their investigations regarding my mother's murder, I would like to know what new discoveries they have made – I want to know if they now know who killed my mother!"

"How can you be so sure that the policemen have been visiting the ashram in connection with Ritu's murder simply on the basis of one visit by them to your mother's memorial?" asked Taanya not quite convincingly. "They could have been simply making a tour of the grounds!"

"Then why was I – the son – and you – the closest friend – of my mother asked to stay out of sight of the policemen during their second visit?" asked Ravi harshly. "Are we being kept away from the police so that they cannot meet us?"

Taanya bit her lip. Her eyes welled up.

"Taanya ji, I am not a child any more. I am no longer the baby you have brought up. I am grown up now and can very well understand a lot of things. I want to know – are you hiding something from me that has an important bearing on my mother's murder?"

Taanya began sobbing softly.

Detective Superintendent Avinash Sharma looked at the computer printouts in Detective Inspector Ramesh Uppal's hands and grinned. "It appears that we are keeping a lot of people around the country awake tonight!" he commented.

It was well past 11 pm and Avinash, Ramesh, Raghuvir and Divyansh were sitting around a conference table in a meeting room in the Gurgaon Police Headquarters. The computer screen in the room was switched on and Ramesh Uppal's e-mail account was open. It was receiving mails, some with attachments, in response to the queries that had been sent out an hour or so ago. Some of the queries had been sent out even earlier.

The printer had been kept busy taking out hard copies of some of the important mails and attachments. Evidence was being gathered – hard action would have to be taken soon enough. The documentation had to be complete.

The fax machine in the meeting room was also buzzing with activity. The incoming messages and document copies were being closely studied.

"Things have come to a head – this is the part of any investigation that I always waited for," said former Detective Inspector Raghuvir Prasad. "The excitement of the climax of an investigation can never be replicated in any other area of work!"

"Well, things are certainly falling into place now!" exclaimed Ramesh Uppal. "The past has revealed its secrets!" He picked up one of the faxes and waved it like a flag. The fax had come from the birth registry office in Bhubaneswar, the capital city of the east coast province of Orissa. "The real name of Swami Satyasivanand is Sanjeev Senapati!"

"And he had a twin brother…" continued Avinash Sharma, taking a satisfied gulp of steaming tea from a plastic cup.

"…whose name was Rajeev Senapati!" concluded Ramesh Uppal, unable to contain his excitement.

There was a deep silence in the room as all four men thought of all the possible implications of this simple discovery.

"I assume that Sanjeev and Rajeev Senapati were – are – identical twins?" asked Divyansh Malhotra after a pause.

"Yes," replied Ramesh. "They were very much identical to look at – right down to their double thumbs on their respective right hands!"

There was another thoughtful silence.

Like a conjurer producing a gold coin seemingly out of nowhere, Ramesh Uppal placed a few photographs which had come in as attachments with an e-mail, again from Bhubaneswar.

There were two small boys featured in the black and white photographs. Both looked absolutely identical. Both boys had two thumbs in their right hands. With a small stretch of imagination you could shut your eyes and visualize the features of the boys growing up into those of the bearded Swami Satyasivanand.

Raghuvir Prasad studied an e-mail report that had been sent by the Bhubaneswar police. "The boys, Sanjeev and Rajeev, were born, fifty years ago, to a schoolteacher working in a school in a lower middle class suburb of Bhubaneswar. It appears that Sanjeev displayed some public speaking skills and a leaning towards spiritualism from a very young age. His parents and relatives singled Sanjeev out for special treatment – they felt that he had a special destiny of some kind."

"This would not have gone down too well with the other boy," commented Avinash Sharma.

"It did not," offered Raghuvir Prasad, continuing to read the Bhubaneswar police report. "The boy Rajeev developed a violent streak – often getting into violent street fights. He dropped out of school at age fourteen, much to the disappointment of his schoolteacher father."

"What happened to the other boy – Sanjeev?" asked Divyansh.

Rughuvir Prasad scanned the papers in his hands and then said: "His parents sent him off to an ashram in Rishikesh when he was twelve years old. The parents were devotees of a local guru who recommended that Sanjeev be sent to *his* guru in Rishikesh for special spiritual training. The local guru made all the necessary arrangements."

"How did the boys land up in Gurgaon?" asked Divyansh.

Avinash Sharma picked up a report that had been sent by the Rishikesh police. He pointed at it and said: "When Sanjeev was around twenty two years old, an American devotee at the ashram in Rishikesh accused him of rape. Shortly after that, Sanjeev Senapati disappeared..."

Raghuvir Prasad shuffled the papers in his hands and said: "Rajeev Senapati was one step ahead of his twin brother in such matters. When he was around twenty one years of age, a teenage girl was found dead in the field behind his parents' house on the outskirts of Bhubaneswar. She had been raped and her throat had been slit with a knife..."

Divyansh made a guess: "Thereafter, Rajeev Senapati disappeared from Bhubaneswar?"

"Yes."

Avinash spoke up: "My guess is that the brothers joined forces after their respective crimes and unceremonious departures from their original bases – and somehow eventually landed up in Gurgaon after trying their luck in other towns."

"Gurgaon was a newly booming township in the late eighties and early nineties," observed Ramesh. "There were a lot of money making opportunities in real estate and land grabbing activities. They must have decided to build their futures here."

"So one became a godman and the other a property dealer and killer!" observed Divyansh.

"Yes. And they appeared to have taken a strategic decision to keep a distance from each other – at least in public!" observed Avinash.

"They were successful in that area, all right!" exclaimed Divyansh. "When I was dealing with him nine/ten years ago, I never knew that Rajeev Senapati had a brother, much less a twin brother who was a famous godman!"

"And I never got to know, during my investigations into Ritu Choudhury's murder sixteen years ago, that Swami Satyasivanand had a brother – much less one with such a shady past!" commented Raghuvir Prasad wryly.

"So how does this all add up?" asked Divyansh to the police detectives. "Who killed Ritu Choudhury? Who killed Jagdeesh Ruia? Who attacked Rani? Who is the Swami Satyasivanand currently residing in the ashram on the Gurgaon-Faridabad Road – Sanjeev Senapati or Rajeev Senapati?"

Some Answers

Ravi Choudhury waited patiently for Taanya's sobbing to subside.

The almost seventeen years old young man was displaying a surprising maturity for his age.

He sat quietly in front of Taanya, a frown creasing his forehead, as he tried to make some sense of the complicated world around him.

Ravi now suddenly found himself in a situation where it appeared that the one-and-a-half decade old mystery of his mother's horrible murder might actually be solved – or so the very recent police visits to the ashram seemed to indicate.

This opportunity – to get to know who had so brutally killed his mother – was something Ravi had been waiting for almost the entire length of his life; ever since he had learnt of the manner of his mother's tragic death as a very small boy.

It was also now clear that Taanya knew a lot more about the tragedy than Ravi Choudhury had previously surmised. He should have guessed this earlier, thought the boy to himself. His mother's closest friend would have been privy to a lot of secrets connected with his mother – before and after her death, now realized Ravi. He would wriggle these secrets out of Taanya, the young man promised himself, even if it took him all night…

Tonight he would find out the truth behind his mother's terrible death, whatever this truth was…

"Rajeev Senapati was released from jail two months ago, after serving out his nine year prison term," observed Detective Superintendent Avinash Sharma. "He was found guilty and jailed in fourteen cheating cases." Avinash looked at Divyansh Malhotra and asked: "I believe it was *you* who was instrumental in Rajeev Senapati's capture?"

Divyansh nodded grimly. "Yes I got that absconding crook captured! As a property dealer, I had become an agent for selling plots in Rajeev Senapati's affordable housing project in Greenfield's in Faridabad ten years ago…"

"…which had been unauthorisedly promoted on government land," observed Ramesh Uppal.

Divyansh looked grimmer. "Yes. I was in such a hurry to strike it rich that I did not check carefully the legality of the document photocopies that the swine Rajeev Senapati produced to convince me and my clients."

Avinash was studying the copies of the nine year old case history that had also been faxed a short while ago from the district court records room by clerks working overtime on police instructions. "Rajeev Senapati had used forged documents to convince his customers and agents. From what we know now, he must have used the clout of his old associate Jagdeesh Ruia and the clout of his brother, the godman, to corrupt the relevant government officials to acquire such forged documents…"

Raghuvir Prasad commented: "Both were obliged to Rajeev Senapati, I guess. Rajeev Senapati took the entire rap for the earlier fraud case – when he was Jagdeesh Ruia's partner. He went to jail – not Jagdeesh Ruia. He even got the complainant murdered. Sanjeev Senapati may have also utilized his brother's homicidal tendencies and murderous skills to get rid of obstacles…"

"Including Ritu Choudhury?" queried Ramesh Uppal.

The men fell silent – was this the answer?

When Taanya eventually ceased her sobbing and looked up red eyed, she saw Ravi Choudhury staring at her stonily. The two sat staring at each other for a while. Then Taanya shrugged her shoulders defeatedly.

"What is it that you want to know?" asked Taanya tiredly.

"Why are the policemen visiting the ashram? Why are they keeping a watch? Have they got some new clue regarding the identity of the serial killer who is supposed to have murdered my mother?"

"I have a feeling that the police think that the killer is right now in the ashram…"

Ravi Choudhury's face went white. "What!" His eyes blazed. "Who is it that the police suspect?"

"*Swami ji.*"

Ravi looked as if he had been hit by an iron pillar. His face was ashen. "What are you saying, Taanya ji? How can they – or you – think such a thing of Guru ji?"

Taanya's eyes dropped to Ravi's right hand. She stared

pointedly at the two thumbs. "*Swami ji* is your father," she stated with a choke in her voice.

"So Rajeev Senapati's main occupation was that of a hired assassin!" exclaimed Divyansh Malhotra.

"It would appear so. He seems to have grown up from an insecure and violent boy, who was jealous of the attention his twin brother was getting, into a homicidal maniac and a psychopathic killer," commented Detective Avinash Sharma. "He enjoyed killing – and if he was paid to do it, all the better!"

Raghuvir Prasad observed thoughtfully: "So, all the apparent mindless crimes of the so-called Gurgaon killer were actually contract killings – *suparis* – but given a common thread of anonymous notes and slit throats to make them appear that of a serial killer!"

"From what we have learnt of the murders of Rajshree Mishra, which was committed in 2001, Geetanjali Mehta, which took place recently, the complainant in the Rajeev Senapati fraud case, which happened in 1996, the murder attempt on Deepika Khera and even the killing of Jagdeesh Ruia – there was always a *reason*, a motive, either of the killer himself, assuming it was Rajeev Senapati, or the person who had *hired* him..." observed Avinash Sharma.

"That explains the gap of nine years between the murder of Rajshree Mishra and Geetanjali Mehta," observed Ramesh Uppal. "The so-called Gurgaon killer was in jail during those nine years – he was able resume his killings only after his release from prison."

"And he appears to have gathered accomplices and a small gang of sorts around him – probably former prison inmates who were in jail with Rajeev Senapati around the same time!" commented Avinash Sharma.

"What could be this monster's reason to harm Rani?" asked Divyansh Malhotra, his mind clouding with the thought of her near brush with death.

"Revenge, pure revenge," replied Avinash. "In fact, I suspect that he carried out Jagdeesh Ruia's murderous instruction on Deepika Khera also for the same reason. To earn a fee of course – but also to strike at you, the person who had got him caught. He wanted to weaken your organization by foiling your plans and harming your employees. He wanted to get at you by harming those you trust. Eventually, I think, Rajeev Senapati would have struck at you directly!"

Divyansh Malhotra shivered.

"By the way," asked Ramesh Uppal, "exactly how did you manage to get the absconding Rajeev Senapati captured?"

"A college friend of mine produced and anchored a famous television programme of those days – India's Most Wanted – do you remember?" asked Divyansh.

Avinash, Ramesh and Raghuvir all nodded.

"When my clients filed criminal cases against me to recover the money which Rajeev Senapati had run away with, I got desperate and sent a case history with a photograph of the man taken at the project launch function, to my friend," continued Divyansh. "He included Rajeev Senapati's story in his programme on dangerous and absconding criminals. A television viewer in Dehradun recognized the man in the photograph that was flashed on the screen, as a recently moved in neighbour – and called the local police. Rajeev Senapati was immediately captured!"

"Enough reason to nurture a grudge against you for nine long years – while he was in jail!" observed Ramesh Uppal.

"To come back to Rajeev Senapati's real calling – that of a killer without a conscience – it would appear that his earliest murder in and around Gurgaon would have been at the behest of his twin brother," observed Raghuvir Prasad.

"You're saying that Sanjeev Senapati hired his brother to kill off Ritu Choudhury after the birth of his illegitimate child, to keep her from talking – so that he, Sanjeev, could retain his holy man image?" asked Ramesh Uppal.

Avinash Sharma got to his feet. "Why don't we go to the ashram and *ask* Rajeev Senapati this question?"

"You know where he is?" asked Divyansh, looking shocked.

"I think so," replied Avinash with a grim look. "In fact you, Divyansh, were the key to the lock that revealed the clue – and equally revealing was Raghuvir Prasad's interaction with Swami Satyasivanand earlier today!"

The other three men in the room looked at Avinash Sharma with puzzled expressions.

The Shocking Truth

Ravi was speechless with shock. When he finally found his voice, he was practically shouting. "How – how can you say such a fantastic thing!" His face was red. "*Swami ji* is a holy man – a man of God! He is above such things! My two thumbs mean nothing! There are many more such is this world – are they all the children of *Guru ji*?"

Taanya's face froze. Her voice went cold. "I had warned you not to be so inquisitive! See the result of your curiosity – you are unable to accept a simple truth!"

"How can I believe this? All along it is *you* – along with all the others in the ashram – who have told me that my two thumbs are a mark of God, that I am blessed to be born in the likeness of *Guru ji*, that I have a golden future because of this mark – in the same manner that *Swami ji* was marked out for greatness!" Ravi shook. "Now you are saying that all these were lies – my two thumbs are simply hereditary…?"

"All the devotees in the ashram told you what they *believed* to be the truth. Like you, they also could not see *Swami ji* in any other light but that of the highest spiritualism."

"And what made you think differently?"

"Your mother told me the truth the night before she died."

Ravi Choudhury buried his face in his hands

"The first time that it struck me that something was seriously amiss with Swami Satyasivanand," shared Avinash Sharma, "was when Raghuvir Prasad was reminding the godman of the detailed information he had received from him about the residents of the ashram, a decade-and-a-half-ago, when he met him as the Investigating Officer in the Ritu Choudhury murder case..."

"What was the problem with that?" asked Raghuvir Prasad with a puzzled expression on his face.

"The godman did not recognize you!"

The other three men in the room were silent for a while.

"Yes, that *is* surprising," commented Ramesh Uppal. "I am also surprised that *I* missed this point!"

"I noticed the failure of the godman to recognize the investigating officer of the Ritu Choudhury murder case but did not think much of it – until..." said Avinash.

"Until?" repeated Raghuvir Prasad.

"Until our next visit when Divyansh stopped in front of the portrait hung on the wall in the ashram and noticed the striking similarity in the features of Swami Satyasivanand with those of Rajeev Senapati," responded Avinash.

"And your conclusion is?" asked Ramesh Uppal, his eyes shining.

"I think I know where to find Rajeev Senapati," answered Avinash Sharma. He began to stride out of the room. "Come on. Let's organize a raid..."

"Your mother was very concerned about the future of her six-month old baby," remembered Taanya, now fully composed. "Ritu had been keeping poor health since after your birth. She kept talking of an early death…" Taanya' eyes began to go moist again.

Ravi kept quiet. He was struggling to digest all the revelations…

"Then, the night before her murder, after a bout of vomiting, Ritu broke down and told me the truth about your birth. She told me how *swami ji* had seduced her – it was not very difficult; the helpless girl had virtually worshipped him – and also informed me that *Guru ji* had sworn her to silence regarding the fact that he had fathered you."

Ravi's hands turned into fists.

Taanya continued with her tale from the past: "Ritu told me that she had been pressurizing swami ji to announce to the residents of the ashram that you were his son and heir – she wanted to secure your safety and future before she died from her health problems – which she thought would be soon. Ritu was very upset that *Guru ji* was resisting her request…"

Ravi stared at his two thumbed right hand and said nothing.

"I was so upset to hear all this that, on an impulse, I decided to go to *swami ji's* chambers and ask him to reconsider his opposition to Ritu's request – I wanted him to know that he could not keep his secret forever!"

"You met *swami ji*?" asked Ravi softly.

"No, events overtook me," said Taanya. "That night there was a mysterious visitor to the ashram – he entered though a secret route which only *swami ji* knew of. I happened to see this visitor's face by accident as he was entering *Guru ji's* chambers, while I was also approaching the door to enter. The secret visitor did not see me. But I saw him clearly as he was entering the chambers of *swami ji.* His – his features were *identical* to that of *Guru ji*!"

Ravi's head jerked up.

Taanya had paused and then continued: "I was so shocked at the sight of this secret visitor – who looked like a twin of *swami ji* – that I immediately abandoned all thoughts of meeting *swami ji* that night. I decided to talk to him in the morning."

Taanya bit her lip. Her eyes welled up with tears. She said: "The next morning, Ritu was missing. Eventually, that anonymous note found in the donation box helped us trace her body," Taanya's shoulders shook and she broke into loud sobbing.

Ravi Choudhury stared out into the starless night sky through the window of the room. "Then who killed my mother – my father or his twin?" he asked in a strangled voice.

Taanya took some time to answer. Eventually she whispered: "Your father had your mother killed – though I think it was the mysterious visitor who committed the actual act!" She drew a deep breath. "I have lived with this terrible secret all these years as much to protect you as to protect myself. I feared for your life and mine, if *swami ji* ever guessed that I had an inkling of the truth behind Ritu's murder!"

Ravi Choudhury's face was a picture of agony. Taanya felt the terrible pain the boy was going through. She felt tempted to stop – but now the dam had burst. She had to complete her story...

"There is more, Ravi – the story is not yet over," said Taanya quietly. "We are now in great danger..."

The Grim Secret

The six police jeeps that had exited the Gurgaon Police Headquarters a short while ago raced through the middle of the night down the winding Gurgaon-Faridabad Road and towards Swami Satyasivanand's ashram.

As they cut through the hilly terrain, the police jeeps passed by the spot on the side of the road where Jagdeesh Ruia's blood soaked body had been discovered.

"How did Jagdeesh Ruia land up in that spot?" asked Divyansh Malhotra.

Avinash Sharma was occupying the same jeep. He sat on the front seat – next to the driver. Divyansh Malhotra sat at the back, with a couple of other policemen.

"My guess is that Jagdeesh Ruia was brought to the spot that we just passed, by Rajeev Senapati's men – and then killed. The idea was to make the death look like another murder of the serial killer," responded Avinash Sharma.

"Then what happened at the Manesar farmhouse? I had

thought that Jagdeesh Ruia had stage managed his escape from there!"

"He had; that much is clear. Jagdeesh Ruia had successfully arranged his disappearance. The e-mail intimation was sent from the same account that led us to Naresh Kumar's body. Naresh Kumar had been killed by Jagdeesh Ruia – not by Rajeev Senapati. The mail id in the Naresh Kumar case was not the usual e-mail account which was in use by the person calling himself 'The Gurgaon Killer'. Besides, there was too much blood splashed around the room in the Manesar farmhouse – it was all too artificial. The struggle and disappearance was stage managed by Jagdeesh Ruia himself, all right!"

"Are you indicating that Jagdeesh Ruia met up with Rajeev Senapati later?" asked Divyansh.

"Yes, I think so. Jagdeesh Ruia had to settle scores with Rajeev Senapati. I think they had a falling out. If Jagdeesh Ruia did not kill the serial killer first, he would have been killed himself. That's why he disappeared. Jagdeesh Ruia was desperate for closure – he must have come to the ashram in stealth in the night to confront Sanjeev Senapati to reveal Rajeev Senapati's whereabouts."

"So what do you think happened then?"

"Jagdeesh Ruia came face-to-face with Rajeev Senapati!"

"I will not let *swami ji* get away with my mother's murder!" exclaimed Ravi Choudhury. "I will confront him now!"

"You will meet certain death if you do so, Ravi!"

"My father will kill me cold bloodedly? Even a monster will think twice before considering murdering his own flesh and blood!"

"The monster downstairs is not your father..."

Ravi stared at Taanya.

"But-but you *just told* me that Swami Satyasivanand is my father!"

"The *swami ji* downstairs is not Swami Satyasivanand. For the last month or so I have noticed a changed personality – almost a different person – in Swami Satyasivanand's garb. It took me quite some time to understand what had happened – until I remembered that incident of sixteen years ago when I almost bumped into your father's twin!"

Ravi's eyes nearly burst out of their sockets in shock. "You mean the *swami ji* downstairs is an imposter?"

"Yes, I think that he is your father's twin – the man who committed the actual killing of your mother!"

The police raid was sudden and shocking.

Of course, the residents of the ashram should have been aware that some kind of police action would be forthcoming soon enough. After all, the police jeep and policemen who had been keeping a watch just outside the gates of the ashram had been very quickly joined by two additional jeep loads of policemen that very evening itself.

The ashram and its residents had been put under close surveillance – and the police were not at all bothered to hide the fact.

Nevertheless, when six more police jeeps suddenly turned up outside the gates of the ashram right in the middle of the night – to join the three vehicles already posted there – the residents of the ashram were quietly sleeping. They were not expecting a midnight police raid.

Avinash Sharma and his team of officers tried to contain the panic. They were partly successful. However, the search of the premises was thorough – panic or no panic. Some arms and ammunition was discovered in the ashram. On detailed questioning, three men in the ashram, including the ashram manager, Swami Prakashjyoti, were found to have police records. They had shared prison time with Rajeev Senapati. Swami Prakashjyoti, himself, had been in jail in a cheating case. He was, of course, not a 'swami' then. He had left jail a year ago – and Rajeev had sent a message to his brother to accommodate his former prison mate in the ashram.

Sanjeev Senapati had, of course, never imagined that, as an insider, his new ashram manager would facilitate his own eventual murder and the taking over of his identity by his psychopath brother.

Yes, Swami Satyasivanand a.k.a. Sanjeev Senapati had been killed by his twin brother Rajeev Senapati over a month ago.

It was Rajeev Senapati who had been masquerading as Swami Satyasivanand since then. This much was revealed by the false Swami Prakashjyoti on sustained questioning. He also revealed where the body of the former godman was hidden.

What he did not reveal, because he genuinely did not know, was where Rajeev Senapati had fled to.

There had been only one resident in the ashram who had fully anticipated the police action. Well in advance of the police raid, Rajeev Senapati had taken flight and disappeared.

A manhunt was commenced on the huge grounds of the ashram and in the surrounding forests. It would, literally, be an uphill task to locate the homicidal maniac who had been responsible for so many murders – recent and not so recent.

It was discovered by the police team that a large network of underground tunnels led from beneath the ashram building into the surrounding hills and forests. One of these tunnels led to a cave. The body of Sanjeev Senapati had been buried in that cave. It was exhumed.

Taanya, of course, asked to meet Avinash Sharma the moment she got to know of the police raid. She repeated to the Detective Superintendent all that she had told the hapless Ravi Choudhury a short while before.

The police team thus received confirmation of the hand of both brothers, Sanjeev and Rajeev Senapati, in the sixteen year old murder of Ritu Choudhury.

When the bundled up body of Sanjeev Senapati was brought down from the hillside cave, Ravi Choudhury was standing near the ashram building. He had watched, his face impassive, as the dead body of the man who had fathered him had been unceremoniously placed in the interior of the police ambulance that had been summoned from Gurgaon.

Nobody could guess what thoughts were going on inside the head of the stony faced young man as he watched the body of Sanjeev Senapati being put inside the ambulance. But Taanya and Avinash Sharma, knowing what the boy now knew, could guess that he was not in mourning...

There were several secret tunnels that led from beneath the ashram building to the hills outside the ashram walls. Most of these hidden passageways were not so secret – a select few ashram residents knew of them. Hence, the police also came to know of them. There were, however, a couple of tunnels which were known to only the presiding lord of the ashram himself – Swami Satyasivanand a.k.a. Sanjeev Senapati. Rajeev had come to know of them from his brother – and had used them, over the years to make his secret entries to and exits from the ashram.

He had used one of these tunnels to make his timely escape to the cave high up in one of the nearby hills.

Anticipating a police raid after getting to know of Divyansh Malhotra's presence in the ashram that evening from the ashram manager – and the conversation his former property agent had had with the police detective in front of his brother's portrait, Rajeev had collected the small bundle of diamonds from the safe in the late Swami Satyasivanand's study and had fled though the trapdoor hidden under the study desk and into the secret tunnel.

Rajeev Senapati did not realize that, in his hurry, he had left the trapdoor partly open.

But Rajeev Senapati was safe from discovery.

Ravi Choudhury, on seeing the police team entering the ashram, had immediately rushed to the study to be the first to confront his mother's murderer. Ravi had seen the partly open trapdoor. He had understood that his mother's killer had escaped from the ashram through the tunnel to which this trapdoor led.

For reasons best known to himself only, Ravi Choudhury had shut the trapdoor and moved the desk slightly to ensure that the secret getaway was not discovered…

Closure

The cave was located very high up in the hills. It had been an arduous upward trek through the tunnel to reach this cave. The trek had taken an hour. Rajeev Senapati was tired.

The darkness of the night was now giving way to the dim light of very early morning. As the faint rays of the sun struggled to make their way through the dark blanket that had been the night sky, Rajeev Senapati stood at the mouth of the cave, high up in the hillside, and savoured the fresh air cruising around the deeply forested and undulating Aravalli hills.

He had been lucky to have escaped the clutches of the police. But he had done it.

Rajeev Senapati looked back into the cave and drunk in the sleek outline of the motorcycle that was parked there, fully tanked up with fuel – and ready to ride him off to a new beginning.

The motorcycle had been kept there in the cave for his use when he needed to move out of the confines of the ashram for his murderous activities. This mobility and his double life had been Rajeev Senapati's great strength – which he had used with great effect to keep the Millennium City, in fact the entire country, in the grip of his terror; the terror of 'The Gurgaon Killer'…

Rajeev Senapati turned and strode back into the confines of the cave. He reached out and picked up from the ground the rucksack which he had brought with him from the ashram. He took out from the bag the food items that he had packed into it. The packed and tinned food would keep him sustained for a couple of days.

Rajeev Senapati drew out the small bundle of diamonds and lovingly felt the weight of the treasure in his hands. He had made a rough assessment of the value of the contents of the bag when he had first discovered it in the safe in his brother's study, after he had killed his twin and had secretly taken over the mantle of the Guru and presiding swami of the ashram.

The diamonds would be worth several lakhs of rupees – enough to give him a rapid and effective kickstart into a new life.

Nepal is where he would now go to – taking advantage of the porous land border that country shared with the province of Uttar Pradesh. Many of his former prison cronies were now located in Nepal – they would help him acquire a new identity and the fresh documents that would go with it. He could pay them well for these services – with the money he would get for his diamonds.

He would then head out west. There would be rich pickings in America. After all, he had no qualms about the methods he needed to use to make his money…

Rajeev Senapati put back the bundle of diamonds into the rucksack in the darkness of the cave and then drew out a shaving kit. He would no longer need the thick beard. In fact, after shaving it off, he would then get to work with the make-up kit which he had brought along to the cave. He would need a good disguise to help him get through the roads of north India and into Nepal.

Rajeev Senapati picked up the shaving kit and a water bottle and walked back to the mouth of the cave. The morning sun had won against the darkness of the night once again – the surrounding hillsides were bathed in a serene light that heralded the beginning of a bright and sunny new day.

The serial killer would spend the day sleeping in the cave – he would make his move in the night.

As Rajeev Senapati readied the shaving kit and prepared to part company with the thick beard that had served him so well during the last month-and-a-half, he gazed down at the dirt track that led to a narrow hill road about a kilometer or so away. Tonight, he would wheel the motorcycle down the dirt track to this narrow hill road and then ride it down, past the few farmhouses and cottages of the rich and famous that were located on that stretch, to the main Gurgaon-Faridabad Road. Then he would head for Faridabad, riding his motorcycle securely in the middle of the night and suitably disguised – and eventually make his way to the Nepal border.

Rajeev Senapati would carry with him to Nepal one regret – his revenge on Divyansh Malhotra, the swine who had been instrumental in his capture, the bastard who had stolen nine years of his life, would have to wait for another day. But that day would surely arrive, the killer swore to himself. The bastard Divyansh would one day, in the not too distant future, be made to lose his name, his fortune, his loved ones, his sanity and then his life…

Rajeev Senapati raced the motorcycle down the narrow hill

road. The speed was not exhilarating enough – but, as the road widened lower down, he would take care of that.

The Yamaha 1000 cc was a smooth mover – it ate up the kilometers without much difficulty.

The motorcyclist began to pass by the gates and walls of the farmhouses and cottages that were owned by some of the wealthy of Gurgaon and Delhi, who had constructed weekend getaways on this part of the Aravalli hills near the Gurgaon-Faridabad Road. As the motorcycle raced downhill, the road widened and improved in quality – the clout of the residents of this hillside had ensured this.

Rajeev Senapati revved up the engine and increased the speed. His helmet was firmly in place – he would enjoy the exhilaration of a high speed ride on his powerful motorcycle on an open road that would be empty of obstructing traffic at this time of the night. He would need to slow down a bit, only a bit, once he reached and entered the Gurgaon-Faridabad Road – the trucks plying on it would cramp his style. But on this road, he was free to fly…

Rajeev Senapati reached his motorcycle to a speed of 90 kmph and savoured the beating of the nighttime air against his face. Another couple of kilometers more and he would reach the Gurgaon-Faridabad Road…

The thick wire was stretched and tied tightly – very tightly – to the two trees on either side of the road, just one kilometer ahead. The wire stretched across the road, just two feet above the ground, and was rigid almost, but not quite to breaking point.

Rajeev Senapati's motorcycle hit this wire at 90 kmph.

The motorcycle immediately jumped in the air and then dropped back on to the ground and then skidded severely, completely out of control, and swung on its side in circles, round and round – and then careened out of the asphalt surface and into the bushes by the side of the road, totally dented, damaged and destroyed by the hard tarmac.

The rider of the motorcycle had been mercilessly flung into the air when the motorcycle had hit the tightly stretched wire at high speed and from the air he fell with a loud thud onto the left side of the hard road, bounced into a tree and then crashed headlong into the bushes and rocks behind the thick foliage.

As the dust and the noise settled – and the night quietened again, a figure rose out of the dense bushes bordering the road. He quickly crossed over to the other side of the road and efficiently cut the wire from the tree using a heavy duty wire cutter. He unwrapped the remaining wire from the tree and carried it back across the road. He then cut the wire from the tree on the left side of the road and rolled up all the wire into a tight bundle.

Ravi Choudhury then cut through the foliage to have a look at the broken and prone body of Rajeev Senapati.

Rajeev Senapati had ended up on a pile of rocks. His body lay crumpled – very much like a broken doll. His clothes were ripped. There was blood everywhere.

When the damaged motorcycle and the broken body were found, the conclusion would be immediate and unequivocal. The killer had been in such a hurry to escape that he had over speeded and lost control…

Ravi Choudhury drank in the scene and then turned to go. A sound stopped him. He whirled around to see the broken body of Rajeev Senapati move ever so slightly. The man was not quite dead. Yet.

Ravi Choudhury stood there in silence for a while. The body moved again.

Ravi bent down and carefully unbuckled the helmet from the head of the almost comatose man. He raised the visor and slowly removed the helmet from the head of the badly injured murderer, careful not to disturb the position of the body lying on the rocks.

Rajeev Senapati's eyes were closed. His nose was broken into a pulp. His face had deep gashes everywhere. The man was barely recognizable.

Rajeev Senapati's arms lay prone by his sides, broken and lifeless. The two thumbs on the killer's right hand mocked at Ravi.

The boy placed the helmet on the ground. He looked around him and identified a large rock with pointed edges. Ravi picked up the rock.

He knelt down before the broken man on the ground.

Then, with the passion of a seventeen year old and the strength of a man much older, a driven Ravi Choudhury, his eyes blazing, smashed down the rock right on the centre of the head of Rajeev Senapati.

The head cracked open. Blood spurted everywhere – a lot of it coming to rest on Ravi Choudhury's clothes.

Rajeev Senapati stopped moving. He was now definitely dead.

Ravi Choudhury took one last look at what remained of his mother's killer and then got to his feet. He picked up the helmet of the late Rajeev Senapati and returned to the bundle of wire and the wire cutter, which he picked up. He went back to the foliage behind which he had been hiding when the escaping killer's motorcycle had hit the wire that Ravi had tied to the trees and stretched across the road. Ravi picked up the bag lying there and took out a change of clothes.

He quickly put on the fresh set of clothes, stuffed the bloodied clothes, the bundle of wire, the wire cutter and the helmet into the bag – and raced down the road where he had parked his own motorcycle, carefully hidden behind some big trees and bushes.

Ravi Choudhury put on his own helmet, which had been buckled to the handle of the bike, kicked his motorcycle to life and raced off.

Five kilometers away, on the Gurgaon-Faridabad Road, Ravi Choudhury turned left into a tiny side road. He cut the motorcycle engine and wheeled it into the bushes by the side of the road. A little into the dense jungle, he came upon the hole he had prepared a couple of hours ago.

Ravi Choudhury dumped the bag with all its contents into the hole and quickly threw in the large rocks that were already lying next to the hole. Once the hole was almost full of rocks, large and small, he drew some foliage and tree branches over the spot.

Satisfied with his work, Ravi Choudhury then returned to his motorcycle and kick started it to life. He straddled the machine and gripped the handle of the motorcycle with both hands – the two thumbs on his right hand gleaming in the reflected light of the full moon.

Ravi Choudhury rode off in the direction of the ashram – now *his* ashram. He would pray at the memorial of his mother first thing in the morning – and inform her that he had fulfilled his promise…

The End